1.49

The Honourable Detective

Also by Jeffrey Ashford:

A Crime Remembered
A Question of Principle

JEFFREY ASHFORD

The Honourable Detective

St. Martin's Press
New York

Library of Congress Cataloging-in-Publication Data

Ashford, Jeffrey.
          The honourable detective / Jeffrey Ashford.
                    p.   cm.
          ISBN 0-312-03363-X
          I. Title.
     PR6060.E43H6   1989
     823'.914—dc20   89-32767
                                                          CIP

First published in Great Britain by William Collins Sons & Co., Ltd.

First U.S. Edition

10   9   8   7   6   5   4   3   2   1

The Honourable Detective

CHAPTER 1

Badger stared through the nearest window at the sea and noted that the mist still obscured the green wreck buoy— so visibility still remained at under a mile and a half—then checked the time; just under three hours before he was relieved. After a quick spruce-up at home, he and Winnie were due to drive over to their daughter's place to spend the remainder of the afternoon and the evening with her and Ray and the new grand-daughter. Winnie, he thought, was the proudest of proud grandmothers . . . The phone rang.

'It's Reg here, Tom.'

'So how's life treating you?'

'I suppose I can't really complain.'

That was a change, thought Badger; even in Paradise, Alldyke would normally have found cause for complaint.

'There's something you can do for me. I'm interested in a motor cruiser, *Cistine III*, which has just cleared harbour; she's an 80-foot Riva with white superstructure and hull, twin whip aerials immediately aft of the wheelhouse, and stern davits which carry a yellow inflatable. She's on charter and the man who's just taken her out told the attendant on the fuel pumps that he was sailing for Peterstone, which'll bring him past you. Let me know if you sight her, will you?'

'Sure. But visibility's under a mile and a half so I may easily miss visual contact . . . Why the interest?'

Alldyke answered dismissively: 'Nothing definite. It's just that I'm wondering why she's going out in this weather.'

Badger wondered whether that was the truth or whether there was cause for definite suspicion? Alldyke was ambitious and eager to gain promotion; he was also a man who, if possible, made certain that credit for a bust was not shared with anyone else.

'Here,' said Alldyke, abruptly changing the conversation, 'have you heard about Lofty's latest?' The story was long, complicated, and slanderous; Badger, whose sense of humour was never offended by gross improbabilities, laughed heartily.

Once the call was over, Badger walked across to the nearest window, one of eight which stretched from floor to ceiling. A hundred and twenty feet below, the sea was calm and moving only gently to a slight swell. To the east, two inshore fishing-boats were making for harbour; to the west, a small coaster, on the edge of visibility and insubstantial, was making her way down Channel. He sighted her through binoculars and identified her from her bulbous lines and Woodbine funnel as the *Mary Whaler*. The last time he'd met her skipper, he'd rolled home at three in the morning, to a roasting reception from Winnie.

He crossed to the radar screen. There was less traffic than usual and for once it seemed that all ships were keeping to their designated lanes and sailing at speeds which were commensurate with poor visibility. It wouldn't last, of course. Before long, a Panamanian would appear, charging eastward up the westward lane at full speed.

He felt hungry. He half filled the kettle which he put on the single gas burner, then went over to the coat-stand on one branch of which he'd hung the plastic shopping-bag Winnie had given him just before he'd left home that morning. Inside were several rounds of ham and homemade chutney sandwiches, his favourite, a large slice of chocolate sponge cake, and a Mars Bar. She believed in keeping him well fed.

He ate, drank a third cup of very sweet tea and then, since smoking was forbidden inside, went out on to the narrow catwalk which ran round three sides of the hut, which was raised up six feet on wooden piles. The air was cold, damp, and lifeless, and the smoke rose almost undisturbed. To the right was a sloping field and in this a large flock of sheep was grazing. Despite the fact that he'd only just eaten, the sight of them made him wonder if Carol would be cooking a leg of lamb for supper, knowing that that was his favourite meal.

He flicked the cigarette stub over the edge of the catwalk and returned inside. On the radar screen there were several blips, but his attention was drawn to two, roughly ten miles off the coast, which were slowly converging. Was one of them *Cistine III* which had headed out to mid-Channel instead of proceeding eastwards as she would have done if sailing direct to Peterstone? Smuggling by sea was still a flourishing industry, in spite of air travel, and it never ceased to astonish him to discover what was worth smuggling. One of the latest cargoes to become popular was tobacco for home-rolled cigarettes. This was sold tax-free from the UK to Belgium, where it legally went on sale at a much lower price than in the shops in the UK. It was shipped back by the hundredweight and smuggled into the UK, where it was sold through pubs and clubs at considerably less than it cost in the shops. It made him wonder who were the real crazies; the ones locked up or the bureaucrats at large . . .

The two blips merged into one, dumb-bell shaped. This did not necessarily mean that the two boats had drawn alongside each other because it was a fault of the radar set (it had been scheduled for replacement five years previously; departmental 'economies' had ensured that this was impossible) that its resolution was not sharp enough to distinguish between two small craft less than two hundred yards apart when at more than five miles range . . . The dumb-bell snapped back into two separate blips which slowly drew apart. It was clear that the boats had merely passed close to each other.

He yawned. Roll on his relief.

CHAPTER 2

Inland, the mist was patchy and at times dense. Ansell changed down to second and drove still more slowly. He was a very careful driver. Recently his nephew, on holiday with them, had asked whether he ever went more than fifty? His reply that he'd never aspired to being a second Nuvolari had provoked the question, Nuvo who?

He reached the crossroads that marked the village of Gresham which had somehow avoided all development. It still consisted of no more than a pub, a small general store, a dozen cottages with peg-tile roofs, and an ancient, gnarled oak. The major road was clear and he crossed and the lane began to twist and turn so much that it must have been designed by 'the rolling English drunkard'. No doubt, he decided, if his nephew were asked if he enjoyed GKC, his reply would be that he'd never heard of the group.

The lane ended at a T-junction and Ansell turned right. A few hundred yards further on was a black-and-white farmhouse for sale. Knowing how much Brenda would have loved to live there, he'd asked the estate agents the price. Two hundred thousand pounds. A sum way beyond his present means, yet he could daydream . . .

The mist lifted slightly and more of the countryside— fields, largely down to grass, copses, hedges, an occasional house—became visible, but its limits remained confused and forms shimmered. Brenda had once told him that in such conditions she again believed in ghosts, as she had done as a child. Were any of her adult ghosts the past? She'd been born into a family of wealth and until her late teens had known more of the luxuries of life than the hardships. Then her father had made a series of disastrous investments . . .

A sharpish right-hand bend cut short his wandering thoughts and he concentrated on his driving. To his right there was a wavy line of pollard willows which marked the course of a stream that normally ran shallow, but occasionally flooded to cut the road; this meant he was nearing the long, shallow hill which led up to Ingleton.

He passed a house with an immaculate, geometrically designed garden in which lived plastic gnomes. Beyond was a large, ramshackle brick building which had been the local mill but was now no more than a distribution centre for animal feedstuffs. A patch of darkness in the mist became a cyclist, travelling in the same direction; he put up the indicator stalk and drew out; once clear, he drew back into his side of the road. Seconds later, a car came round the sharp left-hand bend, which marked the beginning of Ingleton Hill. It was out of control, skidding across the road, and instinctive judgement told him he was on a collision course with it. Without any conscious decision, he didn't brake, but slammed the gear lever into third and accelerated. For one heart-thumping moment it seemed the crash was still inevitable, then the other car cleared the Fiesta's tail by feet only.

He braked to a stop, his hands beginning to shake from reaction as he did so; he heard the sharp noise of metal crunching into metal, a brief scream, and then the more muted sounds of a second collision. He swung round in his seat, releasing the seat-belt as he did so, and stared through the rear window. Despite the mist, he could see that the car had hit the cyclist, to send the rider sprawling, and had then mounted the low grass verge to ram a telegraph pole.

As he watched, the car backed, under an acceleration so fierce that the rear wheels smoked as they whipped across the road and there were more sounds of metal being ripped. He had expected the driver to park and then to hurry across to determine how badly injured was the cyclist, but it was obvious that he had no intention of doing so and was intent only on escaping. Ansell flung open the driving door, jumped out on to the road, and tried to read the registration number of the retreating car. But his long sight had deteriorated— he really needed to wear glasses when driving, but had continued to put off that day—and the mist made things still more difficult. He found the letters difficult to read, the numbers impossible. D three numbers AK and then was it an E or an F . . .?

He ran towards the inert figure which lay half on the road, half on the grass verge and as he approached he experienced a stifling feeling of sick expectation, but there was no gaping wound to shock, only a thin trickle of blood which slowly welled out of a cut on the elderly man's right cheek.

Another car rounded the corner at the bottom of the hill, then braked to a stop when level with Ansell. 'There's been an accident,' he shouted. 'Call an ambulance.'

The driver seemed to hesitate, then said: 'D'you know where's the nearest phone?'

The mill was just down the road, but it might already have closed for the day. 'There's a house a few hundred yards down on the right and they must have one. When you get through, say the man's unconscious.'

The window began to rise as the car moved forward.

'Hey!' Ansell shouted.

Both window and car stopped.

'Have you any sort of a rug I can put over him to help keep him warm?'

'I've nothing like that.'

'Then ask them at the house for one.'

The car drove away, soon to be hidden by the mist.

Ansell stared down at the injured man, wishing there were something useful he could do but knowing that, as ignorant of first aid as he was, the safest thing was to do nothing. The other hadn't moved or made a sound and the grim thought occurred to him that perhaps he was dead, not unconscious . . .

An unladen lorry came to a halt with squealing brakes; the driver jumped down from the cab. 'So what happened, mate?'

'A car knocked him down, but didn't stop.'

'Bastard! You've called an ambulance?'

'The driver of another car's gone to do that and I asked him to bring back a rug.'

'Then I'll shove a couple of sacks over the poor old sod until the rug gets here.'

The minutes passed and there was no sign of the other car. 'What the hell's keeping him?' asked Ansell. 'He should have returned ages ago.'

'Then like as not he's shoved off rather than get mixed up in things. Which means, mate, one of us ought to ring through and find out what's happening. Where's the nearest phone?'

'There's a house down the road. That's where I told him to go.'

'You'll be a sight quicker than me so why not get along and find out if the accident has been reported?'

He drove the Fiesta back to the house and a tall, thin, bony woman dressed in a flouncy and unbecoming frock opened the front door. He introduced himself, but clearly she didn't remember their one meeting. She said that a few minutes before a man had used her telephone to call an ambulance, but that he had not asked for a rug.

'Then will you let me have one now? We're trying to keep the poor man warm, but we've only got sacks.'

She gave him both a blanket and a tartan travelling rug. After briefly thanking her, and promising to see they were returned, he hurried back. Another two cars had stopped and there were now six people grouped around the uncon-scious man. The lorry-driver helped Ansell to spread the rug and blanket over him.

Ten minutes later they heard the two-tone siren of the ambulance as it reached the crest of the hill and began to descend, and four minutes after that it materialized out of the mist and drew up in front of the lorry; the siren ceased, but the blue light continued to flash. Two men climbed out of the cab and one of them went round and opened up the rear doors; a young doctor jumped down on to the road and hurried across to where the unconscious man lay.

A police car, driven by a sergeant with a PC as observer, came up from the opposite direction. The first thing they did was to set up reflector warning triangles, then they briefly questioned everyone present and asked those who were not witnesses to what had happened to move on.

The victim was lifted on to a stretcher and this was loaded into the ambulance which drove off, siren once more sounding. The PC, confident but not cocky, crossed to where Ansell waited and asked him for his name and address, and then for a statement, all of which he carefully recorded in his notebook. After Ansell had signed his statement, he was thanked for his help and told that he was free to leave.

CHAPTER 3

Mill Lane was a horseshoe-shaped close on the outskirts of Stillington. Until the 'fifties, the old windmill had still been in the middle of the field which stood slightly higher than surrounding land, gradually decaying as each winter stripped more boards from its sides and the machinery gathered a thicker coat of rust. Then the mill was put up for sale, which provoked a campaign to restore it. A property company bought the land and although they expressed their sympathy with the aims of the hastily formed preservation society, they made certain that the mill was demolished before any effective move could be made to gain a conservation order. They replaced it with fifteen detached houses of typically uninspired architecture, but which, since none of them ever developed any structural fault, could by contemporary standards be termed well built.

When Brenda heard the car drive into the garage, she left the kitchen by the back doorway and went round the house. She said, as Ansell edged his way between the car and the shelves which lined the wall: 'Mike, why are you so late? I've been getting really worried.' Even after twenty-five years of marriage, she still knew the sudden inner ice when the unexpected happened or the expected didn't.

'I'm sorry, but I ran into trouble on the drive and was held up. I'll tell you about it over a drink.'

The sitting-room was on the south side of the house and it overlooked open farmland that in the past year had come under threat of development. Except for the display cabinet, the room was quietly but warmly furnished; the cabinet, a wedding present from her family, was a rare Chippendale piece with exquisite inlay and neither of them had ever been able to decide whether it was delightfully absurd or absurdly delightful to have something so exotic in the otherwise pedestrian surroundings.

He opened the small cocktail cabinet to the right of the large bookcase whose contents proved their reading tastes to be catholic. 'What would you like?'

'Is there any Dubonnet?'

He searched among the bottles. 'There's enough left for one double or two singles.'

'I'll take the two singles. A refill always makes it seem one's had more to drink.'

He poured her a drink and carried the glass across. As he handed it to her, he thought with deep pleasure how little she had changed since he'd first met her. She'd never been beautiful, her features were too irregular, and now there were lines in her round face, especially around her generous mouth; there was more grey in her dark hair than she was yet prepared to admit; her body had gained an inch, or maybe two; but her inner calm and caring warmth were the same as they always had been and because of them she possessed an attraction that no mature man could miss.

He poured himself a generous gin and tonic. 'I was late home because on the way back I met up with an accident.'

'Oh dear! I hope it wasn't a bad one?'

'I don't think so. A doctor came out with the ambulance and he told the police that the cyclist's injuries to head and leg didn't look very serious. But I must admit that when I first saw the poor devil sprawled out on the ground there was a moment when I thought he might be dead.'

'Where did this happen?'

'Just before Ingleton Hill.' He went over to a chair and sat. 'From what I saw, a car came down the hill too fast— perhaps in the mist the driver didn't realize how sharp is the bend at the bottom—and skidded. It was heading straight for me, but thank God I instinctively accelerated instead of braking because otherwise he'd have slammed into me instead of the cyclist. Which sentiment, I suppose, shows just how selfish one can become! Still, it would have hit the Fiesta a lot harder than it hit the cyclist . . .

'Another car came along and I asked the driver to go to the nearest house and phone for an ambulance and to bring back a rug to put over the cyclist. He made the call, but never returned with a rug. When I told the police they said that that sort of thing happens all the time; people do anything rather than become involved in someone else's troubles.'

'I've read about that happening.' She spoke sadly. To her, it was unthinkable to walk by on the other side of the road, like the Pharisee.

On the night of his call to the Bar—and before the decanters of wine and port had caused the paintings of past Benchers to weave about—Ansell had known only bright certainty.

He would become a successful silk who, in due time, would allow himself to be persuaded to go on to the Bench. Thirty years on, he was head of the legal department (the staff of which consisted of a secretary and himself) of a large company which had moved out of London some years before.

He had had the brains to become the silk of his imagination, but intellectual ability on its own had never been sufficient for success at the Bar; in addition one had always needed luck, a thick skin, and a readiness to use words as a weapon, careless how much they hurt. He had lacked this last, being by nature a compassionate man. Solicitors admired compassionate barristers, but briefed selfish ones.

His work with the company was not hard and it was sufficiently varied in character to be interesting, but because there was no chance of promotion, it was in a sense a dead-end job. Yet it provided Brenda and him with a comfortable life—they'd wanted children, but she had been unable to have any and they had decided against adoption —and he was fairly certain that if now he were offered a second chance to aim for success at the Bar he would not, however shaming this might be, take it because once one had slipped into the clutches of job security one found it had fetters of steel.

The intercom on the desk in his office buzzed and Mary, his secretary, said: 'There's a policeman wants a word with you.'

'OK. Show him in, will you?' He returned the contract he had been reading to a folder.

Mary, followed by a man in a brown, baggy suit, entered. She was bright and breezy and liked to wear the very latest fashions, but had the sense to restrict her clothes at work to those which would do no more than puzzle senior management. 'Detective-Constable Brice, Mr Ansell.'

Brice, just above the minimum height for the force, was

overweight, a fault for which the excellence of his wife's cooking was mainly responsible. Middle-aged, he had a round, full face, in which bird's-nest eyebrows added a touch of humour. He shook hands with a firm grip. 'Sorry to bother you like this in the middle of work. I'll be as brief as I can,' he said in a deep voice.

'That's all right. There's no great rush of work at the moment.'

Brice sat on the chair set in front of the desk. 'It's about the road accident yesterday afternoon, of course.' He reached into his right-hand coat pocket and brought out a notebook, which he opened. 'The first thing you knew was when the crash car came skidding round the very sharp corner at the bottom of Ingleton Hill—is that right?'

'Yes.'

'Would you say the car was travelling fast?'

'I don't know that I can judge because I realized he was heading straight for me and all that concerned me was somehow missing him.'

'That's natural enough! The car hit the cyclist and went into a telegraph pole. As it passed you, did you get a good look at the driver?'

'No, only a very quick one.'

'But you may have noticed enough about him to be able to help us, so will you do your best to describe him?'

'My best isn't going to add up to much. All I can recall is a long face seen in profile, a moustache, and dark hair.'

'What kind of age?'

'Maybe the early thirties; something like that.'

'Was his hair straight, wavy, or curly?'

'I've no idea.'

'What was its colour—ginger, brown, black?'

'It wasn't ginger, but it could have been either brown or black.'

'Can you say what was the general shape of his head— would you call it round, square, or oval?'

After a moment, Ansell said doubtfully: 'If I've got to give an opinion, I'd say round.'

'Did you notice the shape of his ears or nose?'

'No.'

'Or his mouth?'

'Look, there just wasn't time for all that. I don't suppose I was looking at him for as much as half a second and then I was still panicking that we were going to hit.'

'I understand that, Mr Ansell, but what I'm doing is asking every possible question I can think of in the hopes you'll be able to answer some of them.' He smiled, which banished the hint of lugubriousness in his face. 'I think an artillery man would call it bracketing the target. And you're doing fine . . . Were there any passengers?'

'I didn't notice any.'

'What make of car was it?'

'At the risk of sounding monotonous, I don't know. All I can say is, it was a large dark blue saloon. As my nephew would quickly tell you, I'm not very good at identifying cars even at the best of times.'

'You tried to read the registration number as the car drove off and identified . . .' Brice checked his notes. 'D three figures AK and possibly E or F. Have you had any second thoughts about the figures?'

'None. I'm afraid I wasn't wearing glasses and the mist was making visibility pretty difficult . . . I suppose only half a number is useless to you?'

Brice said cheerfully: 'I'd look at it the other way round and say that it's a start . . . Let's move on a bit. Very soon after the accident, a car stopped. Since it must have been following the crash car, the driver could probably help us and we'd like to identify him. Now, have I got this right? You spoke to him and asked him to telephone for an ambulance and to return with a rug. When he didn't return, you went along to the house and found he'd made the call, so it was obvious that he'd not wanted to be further involved. I don't suppose you've any idea who he was?'

'I'm not certain.'

'How d'you mean?'

'I've never met him before, that's for sure, but when I was drifting off to sleep last night, I seemed to remember seeing a photo of him somewhere recently.'

'You sound a bit doubtful about this?'

'I just can't remember when or where it can have been.'

'Well, I'd very much like to have a chat with him so if you should remember any more, let me know, will you?'

'Yes, of course.'

'Then I've just about covered everything and can leave you in peace.' Brice shut his notebook, stood.

'Have you heard how the cyclist is?'

'He's got a broken leg, a cut cheek, heavy bruising, and concussion, but nothing dangerous.'

'I hope you find the driver.'

'No more than I do, that's for sure!'

Brice's christian name was Frederick, but amongst his workmates he was usually known as Ernie, not Fred; few, if any of them, could now say why this was. In fact, the name Ernie had been given to him by Ransome, a fellow constable, soon after he'd joined the force and then it had carried a contemptuous connotation which had since been lost. The name had come from a novelty song which for a time—understandably brief—had enjoyed a measure of popularity and two lines of which had gone, 'And Ernest was as earnest as any Ernest earnestly can be.' Ransome, a rugger-playing, beer-swilling braggart, had found Brice's attitude towards his work and his fellow humans so totally incomprehensible that he had once described him as that stupid, do-gooding, psalm-singing sod. It could not have been a more incorrect description, since in Ransome's eyes both altruism and faith had been signs of weakness; there was nothing weak about Brice and if his standards were high, he enjoyed no sense of moral superiority because of this; rather his sense of humour allowed him ruefully to laugh at himself every time performance failed to match ideals.

He'd not changed as he'd grown older, despite experience, but the nature of the police force—meaning the way in which most members of it viewed their work—had; he was bitterly sorry about this. When he'd joined, policemen, and this included even the Ransomes, had allied themselves with the general public; now they saw themselves as a body apart. The rising tide of violence was largely to blame for that; also the continuous and malignant criticisms of everything they did by the left-wingers, in and out of Parliament. They had come to feel isolated and in their isolation had been drawn together so that they became 'us' and everyone else was 'them'. He often remembered with nostalgia the days when a policeman could think of himself as a civilian in uniform; by nature an optimist, he hoped that one day they would once more do so.

He sat at his desk in the CID general room and began to type with two fingers a report on the Ingleton case. Unless more evidence came to light, he thought bitterly, this was one more hit-and-run that would never be cleared up; bitterly, because the daughter of a great friend had been knocked down by a hit-and-run driver and left a paraplegic . . . Make of car unidentified, registration number at best half noted. The most that could be done, then, was to issue a request to garages to look out for a large dark blue saloon which had suffered damage to its front end . . . The latest administrative catch-phrase was: Priority must be determined on pragmatic grounds. So even had the cyclist been killed, it was unlikely the case would have received adequate attention. There was simply too much crime for time and effort to be spent on a case in which the lack of hard evidence meant success was unlikely.

CHAPTER 4

Brenda loved a well-kept garden and by a subtle mixture of flattery and coercion she persuaded her husband, who could readily name many things he would prefer to do, to help her maintain one. He was digging one of the rosebeds when he remembered something and he rammed the fork into the soil, rested an elbow on the handle, and his chin on the palm of his hand.

She stepped into the open doorway of the kitchen and called out: 'I think the chin up a little for Rodin.'

'If that's what you're after, I'd better strip.'

'Out of compassion for our neighbours, no . . . Clare's just phoned and asked if we'll go there for a meal on the first.'

'Surely we can find a previous invitation?'

'We'll do nothing of the sort. She's also asking the Creswells.'

'Add in the Bladens and my cup of gall will overflow.'

'You're quite impossible and ought to go and live on a desert island; with only yourself as company, you'd really learn how bad things can be!'

'For those few kind words, I thank you.'

'It's going to be dark soon, so are you coming in?'

'I wanted to finish this bed.'

'You'd find the job would go a lot quicker if you didn't spend so much time leaning on the fork.'

His tone changed and became serious. 'As a matter of fact, I was thinking about the crash. I reckon I've remembered where I saw a photo of the man in the other car.'

'Oh! Where?'

'In the county magazine, either last month's issue or this.'

'Suppose you're right, what do you do about it?'

'I'll tell the detective-constable who came to see me at the office.'

'Who will, one hopes, question him and make him feel very small for running away.'

He finished the rosebed and went into the kitchen, where he washed his hands, then through to the sitting-room. He sat, glad to rest his back which was beginning to suggest that he would have been well advised not to have done quite so much uninterrupted digging, and picked up from a coffee table two glossy monthly magazines. On the third page of the second one was the photograph of a man and woman who stood by a table on which were a dozen bottles of champagne in a cane basket. 'Here we are!' he called out.

She came through from the kitchen where she had been peeling potatoes.

'His name's Stephen Poulton and he donated the first prize for the draw at one of the local charity balls. According to the caption, he's not only generous and wealthy, he's witty to boot.'

'It sounds as if he gave the caption-writer a couple of glasses of something.'

'Probably . . . Judging by the woman he's with, the great man has one more asset—he's up to gold medallist standards in bedroom gymnastics.'

The police Escort turned off the road and passed through the gateway on the right-hand side of which was a gatehouse. Ahead stretched a drive, lined by oaks, at the end of which was a Caroline mansion.

'Strewth!' said Higgs.

'What's up with you?' asked Drew.

'Well, look at it.'

'What about it?' Drew demanded antagonistically, his handsome but hard face expressing contempt for youthful naïvety.

Higgs didn't answer. He'd only been working in CID as an aide for a month, but that had been time enough to appreciate the fact that the detective-constable made a point of never being impressed by anyone or anything.

'Never forget something, my lad. There's no one ever gets that rich without kicking everyone else in the goolies.'

'I don't know about that . . .'

'Like you don't know about most things.'

'But there are some rich blokes who do a lot of good.'

'Because they've got cold feet and are trying to buy their way into heaven.'

'I thought you didn't believe in heaven?'

'I don't, but those bastards do when they start to think about their own graves.'

Higgs laughed.

You'll learn, thought Drew, as he braked the car to a stop in the turning circle. He prided himself on being suckered by neither preacher nor politician and always remembering that even the chief constable was merely human.

They climbed out of the car. Seen that close to, the house was obviously very large.

'I wonder what it costs to run a year?' said Higgs.

'A bloody sight more than you or I will ever see,' came the inevitable answer. Yet much to his annoyance, Drew was impressed by the timeless beauty of the house and grounds and he recalled an old man who'd said that history wasn't dates, it was bricks and mortar . . . There was a high, pillared portico and inside this a large, arched wooden door with panels; to the right of this, set in the wall, was an antique bell-pull, in the shape of a fox's head, which had been adapted to work on electricity. He pulled it and they heard the bell sound inside.

'Makes one think of ruffles and crinolines,' said Higgs.

'It makes me think of Dracula,' snapped Drew.

A middle-aged woman, wearing an apron over a flower-print frock, opened the door. She peered at them with her eyes slightly screwed up, suggesting she should have been wearing glasses.

'Detective-Constable Drew and PC Higgs, local police. If Mr Poulton's in, we'd like a word with him, please.'

'You'd better come in, then.'

They entered. 'If you'll wait a moment,' she said. They watched her cross the large hall and pass through one of the two doorways on the far side, then they examined more closely their surroundings. There was dark wooden panelling, a full suit of armour on either side of the huge open fireplace, arms arranged in two circular designs, four paintings in heavy gold frames (one depicting a buxom, naked woman who posed in a manner, decided Drew, that had the setting not been classical would certainly have excited the attention of centrefold devotees), a long refectory table on which were two bowls of cut flowers, numerous pieces of silver both large and small, and an assortment of glossy magazines, and on the floor three carpets which glowed with colour. Just waiting for the TV cameras to arrive, he assured himself.

A man entered and walked across to stand in front of the fireplace. 'Good morning.'

There was a look of smooth success about him and this was reinforced by his off-hand confidence. 'I gather you want a word with me about something?' His time was real money, his attitude said.

Drew knew something about men's clothes and looking at Poulton's he reckoned there could have been no change from several hundred pounds after buying the mohair cardigan, the roll-neck shirt, the beautifully cut slacks, and the Italian shoes. 'That's right, Mr Poulton.' He was careful to make it clear that the time had long since gone when a detective-constable metaphorically touched his forelocks to someone who was influential or rich. 'We're making inquiries into a road accident. Did you witness one at the bottom of Ingleton Hill last Monday?'

Poulton walked over to the refectory table, opened a heavily chased silver box, and brought out a cigarette; he lit this with a gold lighter. 'What makes you think I might have done?'

'You've been named as the driver of a car which came on the scene.'

'Named by whom?'

'Mr Ansell . . . Were you near Ingleton Hill on that day?'

'Yes.'

'And you saw the accident?'

'No. I arrived on the scene after it had taken place.'

'You spoke to Mr Ansell who asked you to go to the nearest house and phone for an ambulance?'

'Which I did.'

'He also asked you to return with a rug to put over the injured man, which you did not.'

'Are you sure?'

'Quite sure you didn't return, yes,' replied Drew scornfully.

Poulton spoke patiently, not angrily. 'What I mean is, are you sure he asked me to return with a rug?'

'That is what he says.'

'Then I'm sorry, but I just didn't realize that. Frankly, any kind of accident always turns me up and I just didn't take in everything he said. I suppose all I could really concentrate on right then was a stiff whisky to steady my nerves. Naturally, if I'd understood him, I'd have done everything I could.'

Drew silently called him a liar, but regretfully accepted that there was little chance of proving this. 'Why haven't you reported the incident to the police?'

'Where was the point? I didn't come on the scene until after the accident had happened. I didn't see anything of the slightest consequence.'

'Surely it would have been better to leave us to judge that?'

'You couldn't have come to any other conclusion.'

'When you drove down Ingleton Hill, was there a car ahead of you?'

'Yes. It had overtaken me just before the hill.'

'Can you say what make it was?'

'A Ford Granada.'

'Was it being driven fast?'

'Since it overtook me, it was obviously going faster than I was, but I can't give any meaningful figure since I don't know what my own speed was.'

'What car were you in?'

'My Jag.'

'Then you won't have been hanging about, will you?'

'Nor, in that sort of weather, would I have been going like the clappers.'

'Did anything about the way the Granada was being driven suggest to you that the driver might be tight?'

'I don't think so.'

'Since he was going faster than you, would you say he was driving too fast for the conditions?'

'Not if he was a smart driver.'

'Hardly very smart, since he smashed into the old boy on the bike . . . Did you notice the car's registration number?'

'No.'

'Or get a good look at the driver?'

'Since he was overtaking he was on the far side of the car and the passenger's head obscured his.'

'How many passengers were there?'

'I only saw the one.'

'Can you say what happened as he approached the corner at the bottom of the hill?'

'He braked and went into a pretty violent skid.'

'Because of the speed at which he was driving?'

'Partly that, I suppose, but also there were a lot of leaves on the road and they may have caused the trouble; the mist had dampened everything.'

'What did you see when you rounded the corner?'

'One car, which had been coming in the opposite direction had stopped; the Granada was visible for a second before it disappeared into the mist; there was a cycle on its side and a man stretched out across the road and the verge.'

'And you stopped and spoke to the driver of the Fiesta . . . Can you tell us anything more about the Granada?'

'There's nothing more to tell.'

Drew mentally checked that he'd asked all the questions. 'Thanks for your help, Mr Poulton.'

'Always glad to give the police a hand.'

The words had been spoken mockingly. Drew was sorry that it had not been Poulton's car which had smashed into the cyclist; it would have been a pleasure to have arrested him.

They left and returned to their car. Drew started the engine and was about to drive off when they saw a Renault coming up the drive. It parked on the far side of the turning circle and a woman climbed out. She gave them the briefest of glances as she went over to the door and into the house.

'Doesn't the supercilious bastard lack for anything?' demanded Drew resentfully.

It had, decided Poulton, as he poured himself a drink, been stupid to antagonize the policemen even if the older one had been aggressive; now that he was rich, he should have learned to look on the police as natural allies, not enemies. The words 'now that he was rich', as always gave him great pleasure. He looked around the room. Several pieces of good antique furniture, five minor masters on the walls, a small but choice collection of Chinese porcelain dishes from the seventeenth century, a Tompion longcase clock, three rare wooden fertility masks from Togoland, Kirman and Shiraz carpets . . : Only a wealthy man with taste had such possessions. It was true that he had not actually collected them, but he had had the sense and taste to buy the contents at valuation at the same time as the house. Since then, both house and contents had greatly increased in value, so it had been a smart piece of business. But then he was nothing, if not a smart businessman . . .

By the age of twelve he had discovered that in England there were two classes, not three—the clever and the mugs. His mother had somehow, and only she knew at what cost, saved a little money and she had kept it—ever the traditionalist—in the kitchen in a tin marked Tapioca. He'd taken the money and with it bought fifty Cuckoo Maran hens because they laid dark brown eggs and mugs were always willing to pay more for brown eggs, believing them to taste better than white ones. Just before he'd moved on from egg production, he'd owned a flock of four hundred and fifty laying hens. Naturally, he'd always charged his mother the going rate for any eggs she had.

At sixteen, a street-trader had taught him certain truths which had been of great value to him ever since; truths that then had been specific to the art of selling fruit and vegetables from a barrow, but which were equally pertinent to much wider markets. Divide apples into two unequal piles and charge more for those from the smaller pile; mugs believe that if something is priced higher and in shorter supply it must be better. Put the good fruit on the top and the not so good on the bottom; extol the top fruit, but sell from the bottom. Short-change everyone; only one in four mugs will count the change. If accused of deliberately short-changing, laugh and joke while repaying; a mug finds it very difficult to believe that a laugh can conceal villainy. Never try to bribe a policeman before he has given an indication of his price . . .

He'd bought a large and dilapidated Victorian house and after six months of working as many as sixteen hours a day had turned the accommodation into nine bed-sitters. In order to make the tenants feel secure, he'd hired a nineteen-stone ex-wrestler to act as caretaker and to collect the rents . . .

He'd formed a property company which after three years had run into trouble and had had to go into liquidation. At this time it had been discovered that a large sum of money had vanished. He'd been as helpful as possible and full of sympathy for the shareholders who'd lost their money, even to the extent of forgiving those who accused him of theft . . .

Of course, his life hadn't been all success; whose was? His biggest mistake had been to marry Judy because she'd been able to offer the one thing which he lacked—a good background. Later, he'd discovered that when one became sufficiently wealthy, one no longer needed a good background to be accepted because even the county families with pedigrees longer than a Cruft's supreme champion respected real money . . .

His thoughts were cut short when Amanda came into the room. Tall, auburn-haired, strikingly beautiful, she had a figure that could wear a sack and still look elegant. When St Augustine had called for his chastity to be deferred, it must have been after meeting someone like Amanda.

She stood in the centre of the room, striking a pose. 'Jean's just said that the men who were driving away when I arrived were detectives?' Her voice was filled with velvet promises.

'Then for once she's actually got her facts right,' he answered.

'So what have you been up to—robbing a bank?'

'Not one, two.'

'Come on, Steve, tell me what they were here for?'

'They were making inquiries about a hit-and-run.'

'You're not saying you've knocked someone over?' she asked, worried about the possible consequences to herself.

'Nothing to do with me. It was another car which clobbered the old boy on a bike and then didn't stop. I just happened to come along immediately afterwards.'

'Then you're not to blame?'

'You sound disappointed. Shall I try and bring a little excitement into your life by bowling over a couple of OAPs the next time I go out?'

'There's no need to get all snarly,' she said, in her little-girl voice.

CHAPTER 5

Brice sat at his desk, which was at the back of the CID general room, and stared through the nearer window. There was not a cloud in the sky and for late September it was warm. Had it been his day off, he and Dora could have driven up into the hills for a picnic. He loved picnics, even though he suspected that there was something faintly ridiculous about a man of his age enjoying them so much . . .

One of the younger DCs came into the room, saw him, and said: 'A penny for your thoughts if they're not too filthy for my Persil ears.'

'I was thinking about the hills.'

'Not worth a halfpenny.' He crossed the room to hand Brice a sheet of paper. 'This has just come in and it's for you.'

The Telex message was from B Division and it contained a summary of the evidence in a case of arson. He put the paper down and thought about the hit-and-run. He knew what the detective-sergeant was going to say—put it on ice.

Except to the victim, it was not a serious crime. Even so, had there been sufficient evidence to ensure the probability of a quick identification of the hit-and-run driver, it would have been worth pursuing; but on the evidence to hand, or rather the lack of any, the task was bound to be difficult, perhaps impossible. And so, since there were many far more serious crimes on the books, this case would have to be shunted sideways into the 'In Hand' category. No one seriously believed that even a tithe of those cases would ever be dusted down and re-investigated, but it sounded better not to have a category listed 'Unsolved'.

So only the driver and passenger of the Granada would ever know who it was who'd smashed into the elderly cyclist . . . Brice pictured Rosie, the paraplegic daughter of his great friends. For her, even the simplest of tasks called for determination and will-power. Yet the driver who'd mown her down was probably leading a normal, healthy life . . . He knew a hatred for the driver of the Granada. Why should he remain free if there were the slightest possibility of bringing him to justice? Who had the moral, as opposed to the administrative, right to say that the old man's case was not serious enough to warrant a full investigation?

Could the driver and his car be identified? Ansell had said that the registration number was D three figures AK and then an E or an F. Since he admitted to poor eyesight over distance, it had to be accepted that the last letter might be neither E nor F, but one which when seen unclearly could be mistaken for either. Brice wrote out the alphabet. He judged that there were eight letters of fairly similar shape; those gave a choice of nearly eight thousand cars; this number, however, could be reduced. Ansell had said that it was dark blue and Poulton that it was a Granada. Only a small proportion of those eight thousand would be dark blue Granadas . . . The Department of Vehicle Licensing could list which of them were, but would not do so because of the pressure of work (or the inbuilt reluctance of any bureaucrat to do anything) unless a priority request was issued.

Assume he had a list of dark blue Granadas. The owners would have to be questioned and because he'd be carrying on the investigation unofficially, he'd have to work on his own. Yet numbers could once again be reduced, this time by logical assumptions. The odds were that the car was owned by someone who lived locally; of people who were involved in vehicle accidents, 72 per cent lived within 20 miles of the accident. Since the driver had not appeared to be drunk, the accident had probably been caused by a combination of excess speed, wet leaves, and a damp road; after an accident caused by misjudgement, not criminal carelessness, the ordinary driver did not panic and flee, he stayed to give what help he could. The driver of the Granada had showed signs of considerable panic—frantic over-revving as he backed, a complete disregard for further damage as the car was wrenched free of the telegraph pole —so that it was possible he'd had special cause to fear the inevitable police investigation. Any criminal feared, rightly or wrongly, that if he became even indirectly involved in a crime, he'd automatically become a prime suspect; a criminal driving to, or returning from, a job had every reason to flee a police investigation . . .

Later Brice studied the list just received from Swansea. One hundred and seventeen names and addresses. He swore. He'd not imagined that the numbers would be so great since the car was a relatively expensive one. He was briefly tempted to forget the whole idea. But he was a stubborn man and so he sent a request to Records to check the hundred and seventeen names for criminal records.

Detective-Sergeant Mumford was determined to make detective-superintendent, or better, before he retired and therefore there were times when he was more concerned with making certain he did nothing wrong than that he did something right. The two possibilities were not necessarily opposite sides of the same coin. There were times when the rules said something should be done in such-and-such a way and experience said that there was a much greater chance of success if it was done in another; he always followed the rules because then he could claim their protection.

He looked up at Brice. 'I've just been in with the detective-inspector. He's received a report from Records, following a request about which he knew nothing which is very odd since it was graded priority. As you were the originator of the request, he'd be grateful if—provided it doesn't inconvenience you—you'd put him in the picture.'

'It's the Ingleton case, Sarge.'

Mumford stared blankly at him for a couple of seconds, then said disbelievingly: 'The old man on a bike; the case I said to put on ice?'

'Yeah.'

He rested his elbows on the desk. 'Perhaps you'd like to explain why you've disobeyed orders in so dramatic a style?'

'It's just . . . The car didn't stop.'

'That's usual in a hit-and-run.'

'But when I thought of the driver getting away with it . . . Sarge, you've got to remember that as far as the poor old man on the bike is concerned, it's a very serious crime and so it should be taken as far as we can.'

'Irrespective of what other and far more important cases are in hand? Priorities must be decided not by the facts, but by the emotional responses of the victims . . .?'

Brice stared into space as the angry words rolled on. Mumford had received a blasting from the detective-inspector and, as was traditional, was passing this on.

At the conclusion Brice asked: 'Were any of the names known to Records?'

'One.'

'Which one?'

'Sam Wright.'

'What's his form?'

'It doesn't bloody matter what it is. This case is on ice.'

'But, Sarge, oughtn't we at least to check him out? I mean, having asked for the information on a priority ticket, it surely would look better to have made some use of it if questions are ever asked?'

'If I were the DI,' said Mumford bad-temperedly, 'I'd

have you back pounding the beat so bloody quickly your feet would catch fire.'

Wright, with his wife, lived in Ackersham, a market town six miles from Stillington which had been lucky enough to escape the degree of development that the latter town had suffered. Their Victorian house was large and double-fronted and it was set in a well-kept garden which abutted the park, to which there was direct access. Neighbours considered the Wrights to be nice people who tended to keep themselves to themselves; it was assumed by them that he had the sort of lucrative job which allowed him to do much of his work at home.

'It's the place coming up,' said Higgs. 'I can see the name on the gateway.'

Brice showed, changed into first, and turned into the wide gravel drive.

'He's not starving, then. And they say that crime doesn't pay!'

Brice pulled on the handbrake. 'Not in the long run, it doesn't.'

'Or you hope it doesn't because that would get values wrong?'

Brice smiled, acknowledging that there was some truth in that.

They left the car and crossed to the front door. This was opened by a tall, fashionably slender woman, who was dressed smartly and who wore several pieces of valuable-looking jewellery. Her expression became antagonistic when she instinctively identified them as policemen.

'Is Mr Wright in?' Brice asked.

'And if he is?'

'We'd like a word with him. CID.'

She hesitated, then finally stood to one side. When they were standing in the hall and she had shut the door, she said curtly, 'Wait here.'

A couple of minutes later she came out of one room to lead them into another. The large sitting-room was furnished luxuriously. Through the two large sash windows could be seen the back garden, with its many flowerbeds and large lawn, and beyond, the park. She looked round the room, as if checking nothing was lying around which could be easily stolen, and left.

Brice, always interested to note what other people read because he believed this to be a useful guide to character, crossed to the bookcases which lined the walls on either side of the ornate fireplace. 'He's a great one for Trollope,' he said, surprised.

'Who isn't, given the chance?'

'I'm talking about the author!'

Higgs looked at the several photographs in heavy silver frames which stood on the grand piano, each of which featured Mrs Wright either on her own or with her husband. In several of them she was smiling and he realized how attractive she could look.

Wright entered the room. A tall man, he was sufficiently solidly built for his height not to be immediately apparent; he was handsome in a craggy manner and possessed an air of authority; his hair was styled, but conservatively, and his moustache was neatly trimmed. He looked the successful businessman the neighbours thought him.

''Morning, Mr Wright,' said Brice. He was always polite at the beginning. 'I'm Detective-Constable Brice and this is PC Higgs.'

Wright nodded before he walked over to a low table and picked out one of the pipes from a mahogany rack. He opened a tobacco bowl and packed the bowl of the pipe, then crossed to one of the armchairs. 'There's no extra charge for sitting.' He sat. 'All right, so what brings you here?' He sounded slightly bored and not in any way worried.

'We're making inquiries about a road accident,' said Brice. 'It occurred just after five in the afternoon on the twenty-first of last month, at the foot of Ingleton Hill. Do you know anything about it?'

'Nothing.'

'I wonder if you'd mind saying where you were on that day?'

'I wouldn't mind, but I can't.'

'How's that?'

'Can you say where you were a fortnight ago?'

'I certainly could if I'd witnessed an accident.'

'And so could I.' The pipe had gone out and he relit it. 'Were you near Ingleton on that day?'

'No.'

'Can you be quite certain, if you can't remember where you were?'

Wright smiled briefly. 'But I can remember where I wasn't. It's months since I was near Ingleton.'

'What kind of a car do you own?'

'A Granada and my wife has a small BMW.'

'Is the Granada dark blue?'

'And if it is?' His manner remained polite and easy, but there was now a look of wariness in his dark brown eyes.

'On the twenty-first, a dark blue Granada descended Ingleton Hill too fast, skidded on the corner at the bottom, knocked an old man off his bike, and went into a telegraph pole. The driver then backed and took off in a hurry. Was that your car?'

'I've already said that it wasn't.'

'The driver of another car witnessed the accident and took the number of the escaping Granada; that number says it was yours.'

'Then he misread the number.'

'He's quite certain he did not and I'd say that a couple of hours in the witness-box wouldn't shake him.'

'Then the other car must have the same number as mine.'

'Can't you think up something smarter than that?' asked Brice curiously.

'Sounds like you don't read the papers. Not so long ago, a bloke who'd bought a second-hand car saw the one ahead of him had the same registration number. Being straight, he reported the fact to the police, which was bad luck for him since it turned out that it was his car which had been stolen.' He smiled. 'The story doesn't hold the right moral for a split, does it?'

'I wouldn't know about that. But I do know that I'd find it very difficult to believe the coincidence could happen again.'

'And you'd probably be right. So let's agree that your eye-witness must have got his facts wrong.'

'We can always make certain if you've no reason to object to us having a quick look at your Granada?'

'Why should I have?'

They left the sitting-room, crossed the hall, and went down a passage which took them past the kitchen—where Mrs Wright was working at the central table—to an outside doorway. Ten feet beyond was a brick-built double garage.

Watched by Wright, the two policemen examined the front end of the Granada, both from above—with the bonnet up—and from below, with the aid of a torch.

Brice stood and dusted his trousers after having spent several minutes kneeling on an old sack and peering up at the undersides of the wheel arches. 'Thanks.'

'You're satisfied?' asked Wright.

'Only that someone made a very good job of the repairs. But I dare say that the lads in Vehicles, having all the right equipment, will make a much better job of the search than us.'

'It's funny how you blokes get so as you don't believe even the evidence of your own eyes . . . That car's never crashed into anything, as they'll be telling you . . . Hang on. Maybe I can help you. What day was the twenty-first?'

'A Monday.'

'On the Tuesday, I took the car in to my garage for a

service; they'll confirm that there was no damage then. There's no one would do the job between late Monday afternoon and Tuesday morning.'

'I wouldn't say that—a handful of tenners can make even a British worker get moving . . . Seeing you've nothing to hide, I take it you've no objection to someone from Vehicles coming along and taking the car away for a proper going-over?'

'I'll not argue too much if it'll keep you happy—there's always the wife's BMW if I need to go somewhere.'

A few minutes later, Brice and Higgs returned to the police Escort. 'He's smooth and clever!' said Higgs.

'But not clever enough to play life straight.'

'Maybe for him that would prove too expensive.'

'Don't start talking like some bloody smart alec,' snapped Brice, with a rare show of sharp annoyance.

'Here, what's with you?'

He didn't answer, knowing that to do so would merely be to make himself sound even more unworldly.

When Mumford spoke to Brice over the internal telephone it was to report: 'Vehicles have just been on to me. There are no signs of recent damage or repairs on Wright's car and in their opinion it couldn't have been in collision with the cyclist and telegraph pole.'

As Brice replaced the receiver, he swore.

CHAPTER 6

Not for the first time, Ansell wondered why it was that if one woke up early and couldn't get back to sleep, one longed for the clock to speed up, yet when it finally was time to rise, one wanted to remain in bed.

'Are you awake?' Brenda asked.

'I am. And in two and a half minutes' time I'm going to

have to find the courage to rise and face the day.'

'Is that so daunting a prospect?'

'This morning I have to attend a conference held by Brooks, the deputy chairman. Pat says that marketed properly, Brooks's speeches would be the greatest cure for insomnia since sleeping pills were invented.'

'Isn't Pat being a bit free with his tongue?'

'Undoubtedly. But he's one of the lucky ones who meet trouble half-way, but never has to shake hands. If I took half the risks that he does, I'd have been sacked years ago. But as the law of natural justice puts things, it's only the poor who get dunned.'

'Are you saying that he really does have a private income and so it wouldn't be disastrous if he were sacked? It's not just talk on his part?'

'It's talk, but also fact.' He sat up, folded back the bedclothes and climbed out on to the carpet. 'His brother runs a very successful family firm and he holds a lot of the shares . . . Must add quite a gloss to his life.'

'Money doesn't buy business.'

He was surprised that she should have employed so shopworn a cliché.

'It's true,' she said defensively. 'Maybe you didn't know that Betty's thought about leaving him more than once?'

'I'd no idea—always thought they got on well together. How the hell d'you know that?'

'She told me.'

'She did! You surprise me. I'd have thought she'd be the last person to discuss her private affairs. But I suppose she talked to you because she couldn't bottle it up any longer and you're something of an agony aunt.'

'That's hardly very complimentary.'

'On the contrary. It's saying that people come to you for understanding and sympathy . . . If I don't stop rabbiting on, I'll be late for the conference and Deputy Chairman

Brooks has never yet offered either understanding or sympathy.'

Ten minutes later he went downstairs where he collected the mail from the letter-box before going through to the kitchen. He switched on the kettle and half-filled a saucepan with hot water before setting it on the electric stove.

He checked the letters; one for Brenda from her brother who lived in Shropshire and three for him. Two of these were clearly bills and he put them on one side—leave the bad news until later; the third envelope, made of strengthened paper and the kind often used for documents, was bulky and the name and address were in block letters. He was about to open it when the water in the saucepan began to boil and he laid the letters aside, put in two eggs, set the timer, got out two mugs and put a spoonful of coffee in each, then dropped two slices of bread into the toaster.

He returned to the bulky envelope and slit it open with his thumb. Inside was a single sheet of paper folded around a number of fifty-pound notes.

Brenda entered the kitchen and noticed his expression. 'Bad news?' she asked, suddenly worried.

'Right now, I'm not certain.' He held up the money.

'Good God! Have you backed a hundred to one winner? How much is there?'

For the first time, he counted the notes. 'A thousand pounds.'

The toast popped up and she removed the two pieces and placed them in the rack before inserting two more slices. 'Well, are you going to satisfy my raging curiosity? Who's sent you a thousand pounds?'

'I'm damned if I know!' He put the money down and examined the sheet of paper. 'All this says is, "Remember the three monkeys."'

'You know what it is, don't you? It's an advertising campaign. There's a new product called Three Monkeys and they're beginning to promote it.'

'Would you call anything Three Monkeys if you really wanted to sell it? And since when have advertisers thrown around large sums of cash?'

'All the time, in one form or another. You've seen the competitions. Give five reasons why our soup is better than anyone else's and if you prove to be the biggest liar you win a car. This is just a different way of going about things and if you stop to think about it, it's a very good idea. Everybody who receives a thousand pounds will shout the news from the rooftops.'

The pinger pinged and the toast sprang up; he brought out the eggs and set them in egg-cups, she put the toast in the rack. They sat at the table.

'Mike,' she said, as she buttered a piece of toast, 'with a thousand pounds we can have the sitting-room chairs recovered and new curtains . . . Why are you looking like that?'

'I was thinking that the three monkeys were see nowt, hear nowt, and say nowt. This money's probably meant to be a bribe.'

'Damn! There go the new covers and curtains!'

From the bed, Poulton watched Amanda, who was wearing a short, diaphanous nightdress, walk across the thick-pile carpet to the nearer window; when she drew the curtains, her body was outlined by the sunshine. He could be certain she was not unaware of the erotic picture she presented since she was a clever saleswoman.

'It's a really lovely day,' she said enthusiastically.

'Then ring up God and tell Him you approve.'

'You do say the wildest things . . . Don't you respect anyone?'

'Only myself.'

'Ask a silly question and get a silly answer . . . Since it's so lovely, let's do something different. Like go over to France for lunch at that dreamy restaurant.'

'I'd rather have steak and kidney pud at the local.'

She returned to the bed, climbed in, and snuggled up against him. 'You're only saying that to tease me, aren't you?'

'In my book, it's you who's doing the teasing right now.'

'If we did go, we could visit the casino.'

'Why bother?'

'Because I'm feeling lucky.'

'You are, being with me.'

'You don't dislike yourself, do you?'

'Never had cause to.'

She let her hands wander. 'But it would be such fun to go to the casino.'

'Haven't you yet learned that casinos are for mugs?'

'What's that supposed to mean?'

'It means that the only people who make anything out of 'em are the people who run 'em.'

'You're wrong. The last time we went, I won over a hundred pounds.'

'And how much did you lose the time before that?'

'I've forgotten.'

'Over four centuries.'

'But now I'm feeling lucky and I'll win all that back and more.' Her hands moved more energetically.

If you were paying for something, he thought, you might as well lie back and enjoy it.

Afterwards he showered and dressed in clean clothes—he never wore underclothes, shirt or socks more than once. He had a dislike of any kind of dirt, which was why he never had either a cat or a dog in the house.

He went downstairs, emptied the mail-box, and carried the several letters through to the kitchen table. Jean, the daily, had left everything ready for breakfast so that all he had to do was plug in the coffee machine and take the ready-to-bake croissants out of the fridge and put them in the oven. When he'd bought Highwood Manor he'd considered employing a couple full time, but had decided against the idea; he didn't want anyone to have the chance to pry deeply into his affairs. There was another reason for his decision. Servants employed full time could be the worst of all snobs.

He began to open the mail. A letter from one of his solicitors told him that the Estafan contract had finally been signed; the other side had thought they were smart, now they'd learned that he was smarter. Two items of junk mail. A couple of dinner invitations from people of little consequence so he'd refuse them. A letter from a bank in Liechtenstein which confirmed the purchase of three hundred thousand marks, to be held on deposit (when the Conservatives had abolished exchange controls, thus rendering unnecessary all the labyrinthine deals it had previously taken to circumvent them, they'd gathered his vote). A bulky envelope, of strengthened paper, which proved to contain a thousand pounds in fifty-pound notes and a brief message which told him to remember the three monkeys.

Amanda entered the kitchen and stood by the table. 'We are going over there, aren't we?'

'What's that?'

'Steve, darling, you're not going to be difficult, are you? Not after I've just been so kind to you?'

'What d'you want—a signed certificate of competency?'

'You really are a—'

'Don't stop to spare my feelings.'

'Steve, please be nice to me. We are going over to France, aren't we?'

'All right. Why not?'

She kissed him. 'You're the most lovely man in the world.' She stroked his neck for a couple of seconds, then moved back. She sniffed. 'Is something cooking?'

'I put the croissants in the oven. They're probably just about ready.'

While they ate and drank, his mind was on the last letter he'd opened. The three monkeys—hear nowt, see nowt, say nowt. A thousand pounds to keep quiet. Keep quiet about what? It could only be the hit-and-run. And the size of the bribe made it clear that the driver of the Granada had a very pressing reason for wanting to quieten eye-witnesses . . .

She did not like silence. 'Steve, you haven't said a word in ages and you're staring into space.'

He pushed the money across the table. 'I was just thinking that here's your gambling money.'

Brooks was bumbling along in his usual style and it was difficult, thought Ansell, to make out whether he was proposing a different course of action from that suggested or referring everything back to another committee. He sneaked a look at his wristwatch. Two hours already . . .

If the thousand pounds was a bribe, then it surely had to refer to the accident he'd witnessed; nothing else had happened to him which could possibly warrant any attempted bribery . . . The police would want the money, the sheet of paper with the message, and the envelope. He remembered crumpling the envelope and so he must retrieve that before going to the police . . .

'You don't agree, Ansell?' Brooks leaned forward until his generous stomach came hard up against the edge of the highly polished table.

Agree to what? he wondered hurriedly. 'Frankly, I was just wondering if . . .' He let his voice die away, as if searching for the right words. His belief in Brooks's inability to remain silent for very long proved to be justified.

'You are wondering about the legal implications of what I've been saying? That is a good point and I'd like to deal with it at some length.'

Ansell's popularity dropped.

*

Brenda met Ansell as he left the garage and she linked her arm with his as they walked slowly towards the kitchen door. 'Was Brooks as bad as you expected?'

'Nearly an hour worse; he suffers from verbal dysentery.'

'Poor man!'

'Poor us, you mean.'

They reached the doorway and she unlinked her arm and preceded him into the kitchen. 'Mike, I've been thinking about that money a lot.'

'No more than I have, I'll bet.'

'You still believe it's a bribe to do with the car accident?'

'There's nothing else it could be connected with.'

'But you only saw the driver for a split second and can't really describe him and although you did your best to read the car's registration number you didn't do very well. So who's going to be stupid enough to try to bribe you to do something that you can't?'

'It's a good question; I'll leave the police to answer it. Which reminds me, before I go and speak to them, I'd better retrieve the envelope which I crumpled up and left on the table. Would you know what's happened to it?'

'I put all the rubbish in the bucket which I haven't emptied yet.'

He crossed to the sink, opened the left-hand door under it, and brought out the gash bucket. The envelope was on top and after shaking off some crumbs and smoothing it out, he put it in his pocket.

CHAPTER 7

They sat on opposite sides of the wooden table in one of the interview rooms at divisional HQ; a cheerless room because it was so bare and the walls were painted in two shades of institutional brown, and airless because the single, barred window was shut.

'This is everything that came?' asked Brice.

'Yes,' replied Ansell. 'I'm sorry about the state of the envelope, but I didn't realize at first that you'd probably need to see it.'

Brice examined the badly creased envelope. 'Posted in London, west one—that's not going to get us very far.' He held it up to the light, then did the same with the sheet of paper. 'Pretty cheap quality, from the looks of things, which means it's probably available through dozens of supermarkets; the envelope's more unusual which might give us some joy . . . The next thing is to give you a receipt for the money.' He'd counted the notes before, but did so again. 'One thousand pounds.' From the back of his notebook, he produced a standard receipt form and filled in the date, time, place, laboriously recorded the number of each note, then signed. He tore off the top copy and handed it across, returned the carbon copy to his notebook. 'Keep that, Mr Ansell, and if the money isn't identified as an attempted bribe, it'll eventually be handed back to you.'

'Then I suppose I ought to hope that I've got things wrong!'

Brice smiled. 'You can hope, but I'm sorry to say that I don't think you have.' He pushed back his chair and stood. 'We'll keep in touch, of course, and thanks for coming along and telling us. It's not everyone who would have done.'

'Not?'

'These days, a thousand in cash would make a lot of people very thoughtful.'

'That's a pity.'

'As a matter of fact, it's more than that. Not that you'll ever get the ordinary person to understand that his own changed standards of honesty can have any connection with the general increase in crime. But that's getting on my hobby-horse, so I'd better shut up.'

When Brice had seen Ansell out, he returned to the main staircase and went along to the general room. Two other, and considerably younger, DCs were present and he had a brief chat with them before he crossed to his desk and sat. He brought out of his coat pocket the plastic bag in which were the money, envelope, and sheet of paper, and put it on his desk. A thousand pounds. Because he'd known the time when a five-pound note was a rarity in a pay packet, a thousand pounds still represented a great deal of money. He put the bag in the top right-hand drawer of his desk, even though he would very soon be handing it to the detective-sergeant. He was as honest now as he had been on the day he started work, but he never forgot the honest men he'd known who'd become dishonest because just once the circumstances had been such that temptation had proved too great.

He looked at the telephone. The detective-sergeant would want to know if Poulton had also received a thousand pounds. He found the local telephone directory on one of the other desks and checked Poulton's number, dialled it. The woman who answered his call said that Poulton had gone to France.

Brice telephoned Highwood Manor again late Thursday afternoon and this time Poulton was at home.

'Detective-Constable Brice, Mr Poulton. Will you tell me if you've recently received through the post a large sum of money in cash for which you can't readily account, together with a note about remembering the three monkeys?'

'No, I haven't.'

'Nothing like that at all?'

'Nothing.'

'Then thanks for your help. Sorry to have bothered you.'

He replaced the receiver. It was odd that Poulton hadn't shown the slightest curiosity; the ordinary man would surely have done so. Then had he received a thousand pounds and decided to pocket it, despite the fact that he was a rich man?

Accept that an attempt had been made to bribe both men and it was immediately clear that the hit-and-run case was far more important than the known facts suggested . . . He went along to the detective-sergeant's room and reported.

'What do you propose doing now?' asked Mumford.

'I suppose I'll have to go along and have a talk with Poulton.'

'In other words, call him a liar and something of a thief . . . Listen to me, Ernie. Poulton's not just another Joe Bloggs, he's rich and he knows people.'

'Which is no reason for going soft on him.'

'I'm not suggesting for one second that it is. Will you bloody well stop acting like you walk a couple of feet above the ground while the rest of us plough through the mud . . . What I am saying is that with a bloke like him, you play things exactly according to the book. And that means, among other things, not letting him think you're accusing him of anything unless you've proof enough to convince a jury even more half-witted than usual. Is that quite clear?'

There was a short silence.

'I've told you twice to put the case on ice,' said Mumford.

'I know, Sarge. But now with Ansell being bribed . . .'

'Goddamn it, you're as stubborn as a mule with feathers between its ears. Haven't you any other work?'

'There's enough on my desk to keep two of me busy.'

'Then take both of you out of here and get on with it and forget Poulton and his thousand quid until you're in a position to prove he's lying.'

Brice left. There was, he thought, one more thing he could do. Show Ansell a photograph of Wright.

Ansell, sitting in the small dining area in the kitchen, read the holiday brochures. 'What about unknown and unspoilt Skyros?'

Brenda hesitated, because of a self-imposed diet, then took another digestive biscuit. 'If you can book a package holiday there, I wouldn't have thought it's either unknown or unspoilt.' She nibbled the biscuit and guiltily wished that she hadn't succumbed to temptation.

'All right. Then three weeks tramping the foothills of the Himalayas?'

'You know how I hate heights.'

They smiled at each other. It was a ritual. He arrived home with brochures for the coming year and suggested ever more exotic or luxurious holidays and she poured cold water on his pipe dreams because she was much more down to earth.

He'd just given himself a second cup of coffee when the front doorbell rang. 'I'll go,' he said.

'It may be Ella with the book on perennials she said she'd lend me. If it is, ask her in.'

The caller was Brice. When Brenda asked him if he'd like a cup of coffee, he said he would.

'I hope you don't mind having it in the kitchen?' she asked.

'Makes me feel at home, Mrs Ansell.'

'Then sit down and help yourself to a biscuit out of the tin while I make some more coffee.'

Later, after they'd finished eating and drinking, Brice explained the reason for his visit. 'As I remember it, Mr Ansell, you saw the driver of the Granada only very briefly and then in profile, but I'm wondering if you'd be able to recognize him from a photo.'

'I don't know. But I can try.'

Brice put a large brown envelope on the table and from this brought out nine photographs, each of which showed a man full face and in profile. 'Will you look through these?'

Ansell presumed that all nine were criminals. The fifth man looked like the assistant bank manager of his local branch and he chuckled; noticing Brice's expression, he explained the reason for his amusement.

'If I were you, Mr Ansell, I'd not tell him about this. It's my experience that people who work in banks don't have much of a sense of humour.'

Ansell looked at the remaining photographs and he studied the last one for several seconds before he said: 'If this man had a moustache, he could be the driver.'

Brice used a pencil to shade in a neat moustache. 'And now?'

'I think it probably is he. But I couldn't swear that it is.'

'Fair enough.'

'Are we allowed to know anything about him?'

'Not at the moment, I'm afraid.'

CHAPTER 8

Dora Brice was as overweight as her husband and for the same reason; and like him, she often said she must diet but never did. Even when a young woman, her square, strong-jawed face had suggested severity and middle age had added to that impression, but although she could be as sharp as needs be, her character was kind rather than acerbic.

She was a compulsive knitter; her two sons and their wives received pullovers every year and their tactful references to shelves laden with her work went unheeded. She looked at her husband as her fingers continued to ply the needles. 'Fred, you're not watching, so why not turn off?'

'I am really; just thinking.' Brice looked at the television and was surprised to discover that the snooker table had been almost cleared of balls.

'Is something the matter?'

'It's only a case where I can't see which way to turn.'

She reached the end of a row and changed the knitting from one hand to the other. She wondered yet again why he so often worried about things over which he had absolutely no control. She respected him for his standards, but wished these could have been more realistic for the world in which he had to live and work. 'Want to talk about it, love?'

The game of snooker finished and he switched off the set with the remote control. 'I'm certain a man was driving a hit-and-run car which was damaged in the collision, yet his car's been inspected by Vehicles and they swear it's never been in any accident.'

'So it obviously wasn't him, whatever you think.'

'Then why does all the rest of the evidence name him?'

She finished a row and then used the tip of the free needle to count the number of completed rows. When he'd said it was a hit-and-run, she'd understood. If Rosie had been their own daughter, he could not have been more upset by the accident. She sometimes wondered why he, a man whose emotions were open to so much hurt, had chosen to join the police force. Perhaps he'd never thought about that side of things in time; perhaps he'd mistakenly believed that he could become hardened to others' tragedies.

Brice spoke, as much to himself as to her. 'If his car's never been in an accident, then it wasn't the hit-and-run one. But the registration number fits; with his record, he's more than likely to have had a pressing reason for not wanting to be questioned; the photographic identification is passable . . .' He became silent.

After three more rows, she looked up at the carriage clock on the mantelpiece. 'It's getting late. We'd better go to bed.'

The largest of the three bedrooms faced the small back garden and they were untroubled by noise from the busy road. They changed into pyjamas—she had worn a night-dress only until three months' pregnant with her first child; comfort before glamour—and climbed into the double bed. She enjoyed reading before going to sleep, but he did not and he turned on to his right-hand side to avoid her light. Perversely, his mind immediately became more active.

Years of work had taught him that life was full of coincidences, so that it was feasible that although it seemed Wright must have been the hit-and-run driver, the evidence was really proving it had been someone else . . . Yet those years of work had developed in him an instinct for knowing where the truth lay and he had become convinced that it had been Wright's car. If something was impossible, how did it become possible? It couldn't. Then reverse the question. If something had happened, what would make it seem that it could not have done? . . . Wright was a professional, which meant among other things that he had learned to identify possible future trouble. It had had to be a possibility that the number of his car had been taken, since he had seen the Fiesta, and in this case the police would be along to examine it for signs of the impact with the cyclist and the telegraph pole and no matter how skilfully repairs were carried out, the fact that they had been could never be completely concealed. Then the only way of escaping detection must be . . . Of course! To produce as his a car which had not been in a collision; in other words, an identical Granada with the registration number of his and perhaps, as an added insurance, the same engine number . . .

'What is it?' she asked.

'What's what?'

'You've just kicked me.'

'Sorry. I was thinking.'

'Sleeping would do you a sight more good.'

The sergeant who worked on the national register of stolen cars said over the telephone: 'You're after a dark blue Granada, less than eighteen months old, with light fawn upholstery, stolen during the night of the twenty-first of last month? . . . It could take a bit of time, so I'll ring you back.'

Brice replaced the receiver. He stared with dislike at the typewriter in front of him and into which he had threaded a T21 form. Why couldn't the high-ups ever realize that a policeman could either sit at his typewriter, filling in forms, or he could be out and about doing his job, but he couldn't do both . . .

The sergeant rang him back. 'At a time unknown on the night of the twenty-first, a dark blue Granada with fawn upholstery was nicked from a parking bay in Alfriston Street in Hanwell, London. That's the only blue Granada on the list, in fact, until the night before last when another went in Southgate. D'you want the details of that one?'

'No, thanks; it's after the time that interests me. The Alfriston one hasn't turned up?'

'Not so much as the smell of its exhaust. Ten to one it was on the Continent within twelve hours of its being nicked.'

After the call was over, Brice settled back in his chair and stared the length of the room at the board on which were photographs with requests for identification of people in them. He didn't need anyone else to point out how tenuous was any present link between Wright and the Alfriston Street Granada, yet he was convinced one was there. Something about the second stolen Granada niggled his mind for a second, but then he forgot about it as he pondered the best way of persuading Mumford to order a second inspection of Wright's car.

'Here we are,' said Brice, as he turned the wheel and the car swung into the drive of Fairlands.

'What's his form?' asked the sergeant from Vehicles.

'Not as much as it ought to be, that's for sure, but apart from the usual beginnings there's robbery with violence and a blackmail which could never be tied tightly enough around his neck. He's cool and smart, but not quite good enough to climb to the top of the dung heap.' He switched off the engine.

Wright opened the front door. 'You're back, are you? What's the problem this time?'

'The same as last,' replied Brice. 'So if it's all the same to you, we'd like another look at your Granada.'

'You're not the only one!'

'How's that?'

Wright's voice rose. 'You're not saying you don't bloody know it disappeared when me and the wife were at the cinema? I reported it stolen. Communications been fouled up, have they?'

Brice swore under his breath; the look the sergeant gave him suggested swearing of an even more vigorous nature.

'So there's nothing I can do for you, is there?'

He'd been outsmarted, thought Brice tiredly. But then maybe it didn't take much to do that.

Poulton looked down at the sheet of figures which lay on the large partners' desk. If the figures were accurate, someone in the Frith deal was trying to screw him. It would prove to be an expensive attempt . . .

Amanda entered the library, wearing a very tight-fitting catsuit in glow colours—it could have looked ridiculous, in fact it excited. A man visualized his hands sliding along the smooth curves . . . It was a grossly unfair fact of life, he thought, that almost anything could arouse a man's lust while a woman's responded only to money or love.

'Darling, you look as if something nasty's happened,' she said, as she crossed the room.

'Something bloody nasty is likely to happen to whoever's trying to be too smart.'

She sat on the edge of the desk, uncertain what to do or say next. When he was in a bad temper, he became almost impossible.

'D'you want something?' he demanded.

'I'm bored.'

'What's wrong with the telly?'

'I've a better idea. Let's go to the country club for lunch.'

'Jean said she'd fixed something.'

'And I've seen what she's fixed. Cold meat again. She seems to think we can live on ham and salami.'

'If you'd learn to cook, we wouldn't have to try.'

'I'm a very good cook.'

He laughed sarcastically.

'Steve's being very beastly to Mandy,' she said, in her little-girl voice. 'It wasn't Mandy's fault that the sauce was burned last time.'

He put the sheet of figures into a folder, stood, and went over to a filing cabinet, which he carefully locked after putting the folder in the third drawer.

'Mandy would so love Stevie to take her out to lunch.

Sometimes her little-girl talk infuriated him but strangely, considering his previous mood, it was not so now. He returned to the chair and sat. 'All right, we'll go and nosh at the country club.' It amused him to explore another's weaknesses, even when they were not dissimilar to his own. It was smart to eat at the country club and there was nothing she liked more than to be seen to be doing the smart thing . . .

The telephone rang. The caller was brief. 'If you stay stupid, you're going to get hurt. If a couple of monkeys won't keep you from talking, a cutter will.'

He replaced the receiver. A couple of monkeys was ancient slang for a thousand pounds; there was also the connection with the three wise monkeys. He'd once seen a man who'd been worked over by an artist with a knife and if there'd been a square inch of undamaged flesh, he'd missed it.

He stood and walked over to the nearer window, past shelves of leather-bound books which he'd never read and never would. Threats came cheaply. But this one had been businesslike and undoubtedly needed to be taken seriously . . . Why threaten him when he'd not told anyone anything? Obviously because the driver of the first car must have been blabbing to the police and their inquiries had alerted the villains . . . He balled his right fist and slammed it into the palm of his left hand. Mugs were always causing trouble because they were too stupid even to realize where their best interests lay.

CHAPTER 9

There were times when Ansell's work was not solely legal in character and then his standing orders were to liaise with Public Relations to make certain the public image of the company would not be adversely affected by the proposed course of action. These were orders he enjoyed carrying out because the members of PR were iconoclasts who refused to view the company and those who worked for it with the reverence the company expected.

He left the department still smiling at the memory of a limerick which lampooned the pendantic chairman and took the lift up to his floor. Mary, working at a word processor, was wearing a blouse that plunged and when she leaned forward it was virtually impossible not to observe closely how deeply it plunged.

'There've been two phone calls for you, Mike,' she said. 'The first was from Mr Leverbridge. He wanted to know if clause eight in the contract can be changed slightly so that it won't be quite so specific?'

'Give him an inch and he'll be in Australia. No change.'

'He said would you ring him back as soon as possible and discuss the matter.'

'And have to waste half an hour persuading him I won't agree to what he wants? You get on to him and say that clause eight stays as it is, down to the last comma. Who was the other call from?'

'A man who wouldn't give his name but said he'd call again.'

'Doesn't sound as if it can be important.' He opened the

folder he was carrying. 'Type this lot out quickly, will you?' He placed four sheets of paper on top of the VDU. 'It's for limited circulation, so that's ten copies. And for heaven's sake, this time remember to make certain one reaches the chairman's office.'

She said indignantly: 'He had one last time, whatever his old cow of a secretary says.'

'Convince him of that, not me.'

He went through to his office and sat and thought about the PR man who was off to California for a three weeks' holiday to see his brother. Ansell visualized an impossibly bright and colourful land in which Brenda was with him . . .

The phone tinkled to show there was a call for him. He lifted the receiver. A man said: 'If you stay stupid, you're going to get hurt. If a couple of monkeys won't keep you from talking, a cutter will.' The connection was cut.

His first reaction was to treat the call as having been made by a drunk or a druggy. But then he remembered that 'monkey' was a slang term for a sum of money and a check in a dictionary showed this to be five hundred pounds.

He knew a growing sense of indignation—which he sensed was at least in part fuelled by fear. He'd always led a law-abiding life and therefore he should have been insulated from vicious threats . . .

Brice spoke to Ansell in a different interview room from the previous occasion, although Ansell was unaware of that fact; both rooms were similar in size and appearance.

'It's monstrous that anyone can make a threat like that over the phone,' he said.

Brice tapped on the table with his fingers. He'd learned long ago that there were two kinds of people in the world, those who had been taught that life was lived in a jungle and those who could still believe that it was lived on open, sunny plains. 'How would you describe the man's voice—educated, uneducated, high-pitched, deep?'

'He was speaking for so short a time it's difficult to judge.
I suppose I'd call it husky and rather uneducated.'

'Did he have any sort of an accent?'

'I don't remember one.'

'Frankly, Mr Ansell, there's nothing much we can do
about it for the moment. But if you should receive another,
keep the man talking for as long as possible and listen for
anything in his voice that might help to identify it; even his
choice of words might be relevant.'

'You think there will be another call from him?'

'Let's say that it has to be a possibility.'

'Then you believe I should take the threat seriously?'

'Yes, I do.'

'But where's the point of his making threats when I've
told you all I know?'

'If there's a court case, you'll be required to go into the
witness-box to testify and obviously your evidence will be
vital to the prosecution. If you could be persuaded to alter
it, the prosecution's case would collapse.'

'He really thinks he can frighten me into not telling the
truth?'

'Undoubtedly, he hopes to.'

'Then he's going to find he's out of luck.'

'I'm glad to hear that.' Brice paused, then said: 'I don't
mean to alarm you, but do make certain that you take a few
elementary precautions for your own safety. Keep away
from anywhere that's deserted, make sure your house is well
locked up and don't open the door to anyone you don't
know until you've checked they're who they claim to be . . .
All that sort of thing.'

'You're saying . . .'

'All I'm really saying is, do what anyone sensible does
these days.'

'Because nowhere's safe?'

'Because virtually anywhere can become unsafe.' Brice
stood. 'Thanks for coming along and telling me about what

happened. And do remember to take those elementary precautions for your safety.'

After saying goodbye, Brice made his way up to the CID general room. Forty years ago, he thought, Ansell's attitude would not have been naïve, now it was and it dated him more accurately than his face. Why was innocence so vulnerable? In reality, had evil always been stronger than good?

Once seated at his desk, he dialled Poulton's telephone number. 'DC Brice here, Mr Poulton. I'm wondering if you've recently received a threat over the phone?'

'No, I haven't.'

He waited, but when nothing more was said he thanked the other and rang off. Once again, a complete lack of curiosity on Poulton's part.

Ansell handed a glass of fino to Brenda.

'It's George's birthday next week,' she said. 'I thought we might give him that book on archæology which was so well reviewed last Sunday.'

'That's an idea.'

'A good or a bad one?'

'Good, of course.'

'I just wondered. You sounded as if you weren't certain which it was.'

He cleared his throat. 'To tell the truth, I was thinking more about a phone call I had at the office. A man threatened me if I didn't keep quiet about the hit-and-run.'

'Oh my God!'

'Of course I went straight to the police and told them.'

'What did they say?'

'That there's nothing can be done about it now, but if there's another call I'm to keep the man talking for as long as I can and to listen for any peculiarities in his voice or use of words. And Brice did say that we ought to make certain that from now on we take elementary precautions over our own safety.'

'What exactly does that mean?'

'According to him, don't go anywhere that's deserted, keep the house securely locked, don't let anyone in until absolutely certain who he is.'

'Then he thinks the phone call was serious?'

'Not really, no.'

'Mike, he'd not have talked like that if he didn't.'

'It was more a case of telling us to observe all the precautions which anyone of reasonable common sense does these days.'

She said belligerently: 'I'm not a Victorian virgin, eager to faint, so tell me the truth.'

'That is near enough exactly what he did say to me. The only thing is . . . Well, frankly I did gain the impression that he reckoned things were a bit more serious than he wanted to admit.'

'If that's so, what are the police going to do about it?'

'As I said, there's nothing they can do for the moment.'

'Why not?'

'Unless they can identify the phone caller, what can they do?'

'Surely by now they've traced the driver of the hit-and-run car? They can question him.'

'My impression is that they haven't identified him yet.'

'Even so, there must be something . . .' She became silent as she realized that she'd fallen into the trap of believing that there had to be a solution to every problem.

He spoke more cheerfully. 'I'm sure that if the detective had thought things really could become nasty, he'd have been more concerned than he obviously was.'

She forbore to point out that only a moment ago he had said that it had seemed as if Brice did regard the threat as a serious one. He was trying to protect her as Brice had tried to protect him. Now she must appear to accept his reassurance. Each of them encouraging the other to shut his eyes to the unwelcome. But then wasn't much of life like that?

CHAPTER 10

In recent years Ansell had come to prefer an evening spent at home to one spent out, unless celebrating an anniversary or in the company of close friends; if asked to define hell, his answer would have been a cocktail party given by a successful merchant banker. Occasionally, however, he had no choice in the matter but was ordered by the company to help entertain visiting businessmen. The form of that entertainment never varied; cocktails and dinner at the Bell, a restaurant at the north end of the High Street, famous for the quality of its food and the size of its bills.

It was just after 11.15 when the party of seven left the Bell and walked down High Street to the Red Lion Hotel. That late at night, Stillington was a town that was largely asleep—even the discothèque only opened on Friday and Saturday nights—and they had the pavement to themselves, which was as well because the five Japanese had enjoyed the whisky, the wines, and the cognac. Eventually, however, the hotel was reached and good nights were said.

'By God, they can drink!' said Griffiths admiringly, as they walked away. 'I shudder to think what Accounts are going to say when I put the chits in.'

'They'll probably suspect you of having broadened the entertainment,' said Ansell.

'How d'you mean?'

'Broads—women.'

'Gawd! Your sense of humour gets worse . . . In any case, how would you ever find a woman at this time of night in Stillington?'

'Ask the concierge at the Red Lion for a telephone number.'

'You reckon?'

'That's part of a concierge's job.' Ansell found that he was not enunciating his words as clearly as he would have liked. While he'd been abstemious where the cocktails and cognac were concerned, he had been far from so with the Château Frey-Latour. He must, he instructed himself, steady up before he reached home; Brenda would have little toleration for his insobriety after a dinner to which she had not been invited.

Griffiths came to a stop. 'I wonder if you're right? Are you speaking from experience?'

'Indeed. But let me make it perfectly clear, not from my own.'

'And that was here, in Stillington?'

'No, but in a town exactly like this. Remember Confucius. In pleasure, man in country inn all same as man in palace.'

'Tell you what, let's go back and see just how right you are?'

'And risk destroying the illusion?'

'I don't know what the hell you're on about now.'

'In matters like this, imagination is always to be preferred to reality. Leave things untested and we can picture a concierge with the ability to summon up Cleopatra; question him closely and perhaps we'd discover that he's incapable of even supplying a suburban scrubber.'

'You're nothing but bloody words,' said Griffiths angrily, as he resumed walking.

It seemed, decided Ansell, that Griffiths's annoyance was caused more by the fact that he was refusing to test the concierge's ability as a procurer than by his alcoholic verbosity.

Griffiths's Renault was near the pay-booth of a council car park and at night the booth was unmanned, but above a flap was a notice asking motorists to drop in 50p. He drove straight past.

Beyond the church and divisional police HQ, they turned left into Raymond Street, continued down this to the new roundabout and crossed the bridge which ran over railway tracks. A mile and a half further on the headlights picked out a T-junction, backed by oaks, which marked the beginning of the countryside. 'You don't mind walking from here, do you?' said Griffiths, as he braked to a halt. 'It's late, so I want to get home as soon as possible.'

He would, thought Ansell, have been very much later if they'd returned to speak to the concierge. So this was a spiteful gesture which in turn meant that he really had wanted a woman. Ansell tried to picture Griffiths's wife and failed.

Once on the pavement, he said: 'Thanks for bringing me this far.' He realized as soon as he'd spoken that his words had been too slurred for the intended irony to be apparent.

As the Renault drove off, he began to walk towards the close. He must have heard the car before it neared him, but his wine-filled mind only recorded its approach at the last moment. He swung round and headlights blinded him. For an eternity he was paralysed, then self-preservation asserted itself and he began to run. He'd taken only one pace when a blow to his legs sent him flying to land on the road with a sickening thump. He managed to recover sufficiently to try to read the car's numberplate, but the car was by now some way away and weaving and letters and numbers were a meaningless jumble. Then the car rounded a corner to go out of sight.

Another car came along and braked violently as its headlights picked him out. He heard hurried footsteps and saw a pair of legs appear in the beams. A man, voice high from worry, asked him if he was all right. He suppressed an impulse—a product of shock and drink—to answer that he was fine, he just lay in the road whenever he had the chance.

CHAPTER 11

Brice noted that Brenda was holding her husband's hand, confirming that she—a woman who seldom overtly showed her affection—was far more deeply worried than her composed manner might suggest. 'Mr Ansell, have I got this right—you didn't hear anything until the car was almost on you, so you can't say whether it was parked nearby?'

'No, I can't.'

'You'd spent the evening at the Bell?'

'I and the deputy head of sales were entertaining a small group of Japanese.'

'Then I imagine you'd had a fair amount to drink?'

'If you're asking me if I was tight, the answer's no. But neither was I stone cold sober.'

'What does it matter how much he'd had to drink?' demanded Brenda.

Brice answered quietly. 'Because if your husband had been completely sober and obviously in full control of his senses, the fact that he didn't hear anything until the last moment suggests the car was travelling at speed; if he was partially under the influence, he could have missed hearing it start up.'

'I still don't see the significance.'

'In the first instance, the driver might simply have been going too fast, for one reason or another; in the second, he could have been parked and waiting for the chance to run your husband down.'

She flinched.

'The car, you say, Mr Ansell, was weaving as it drove off. Normally, one would say that that points to a drunken driver, here it could mean that the driver was doing his best to prevent anyone reading the registration number. But against that, if the driver was working on a contract on you, he'd have used a stolen car in which to keep watch and seize a chance if one turned up and he wouldn't really have been bothered if anyone did read the number because he'd have changed cars long before the police could act.'

She said: 'Doesn't all that merely mean that you don't know whether it was deliberate?'

'Yes, I'm afraid it does.'

'But you've got to know. If someone was trying to kill Mike, you must do something.'

That sad delusion, thought Brice, that the innocent could always be protected from the guilty.

'I'm sure it was just a case of drunken driving,' said Ansell.

Brice waited, but when nothing more was said, he stood. 'I'll be getting along now . . . Mr Ansell, it would be a very good idea if you'd remember what I told you before—keep away from deserted places.'

'He was only walking home because I'd had the car to visit an old schoolfriend,' said Brenda. 'I'll make certain that doesn't happen again.'

'Good. Until we've cleared things up, it would probably be much the best if your husband doesn't walk around the local roads at night.'

'You *are* going to clear them up, then?'

'We'll do our very best, I can promise you that.'

Ansell accompanied Brice to the front door and watched him walk down to the gate, then closed the door and, a trifle self-consciously, slid home the bolts. When he turned, it was to see Brenda in the doorway of the sitting-room. 'I'm frightened,' she said.

He spoke with bluff confidence. 'There's honestly no call to be.'

'If you'd been killed . . .'

'I wasn't. And if I'd been sober, I'd have heard the car

before I started to cross the road and none of this would have happened.'

'Wouldn't it? What about that threat over the telephone?'

'The man talked about using a knife, not running me down with a car.'

'That's a lousy piece of logic. You're doing everything you can think of to try and stop me worrying. But can't you see, Mike, that that makes me worry even harder because I know that if you're trying that hard, you must really be worried.'

He spoke lightly. 'It seems to me that when it comes to lousy logic, you're not doing at all badly!'

'Will you stop being frightfully stiff upper-lip. I'm scared and your trying to joke about things doesn't stop that, it only makes me want to hit you for being so infuriating.' She came forward and gripped him.

Detective-Sergeant Mumford jingled some coins in his right-hand pocket as he stood by the window in his office. 'Then it looks like a straightforward case of drunken driving, doesn't it?'

'On the face of things I suppose it does,' agreed Brice slowly. 'But I still think that in fact the evidence is ambiguous . . .'

'You'd find the alphabet ambiguous. Log it as drunken driving, identification impossible through lack of hard evidence.'

'Sarge, I've already entered it as attempted murder.'

'You've what?'

'Because of that telephone threat.'

Mumford went over to his desk and sat. 'With you on the strength, who needs normal cock-ups? You've logged it as attempted murder, so now we're stuck with it and small chance of ever moving it over to the cleared-up column? Goddamn it, you're acting so dumb you'd take a footwarmer down to Hell. When the old man hears about this he's going to blow his top . . . When are you due to retire?'

'In about five years.'

'You may not have to wait that long . . . How the devil am I going to square this with the old man? A simple drunken driving with no real harm done, ending up in serious crime!'

The fact that this case might now swell the number of unsolved crimes in the division, thought Brice bitterly, weighed far more heavily with Mumford than that listing it as a serious crime ensured that it received greater attention and through this the Ansells might be saved from further harassment.

'Here we are,' said Higgs, as he turned into the drive of Highwood Manor.

'Quite a place,' observed Brice.

'I came here before with Alf; he reckons it's just a barracks.'

'Don't you ever forget . . .' Brice became silent. It went against his nature to criticize a fellow DC.

'Forget what?'

'That everyone sees things differently.' From an old fool like me, he was tempted to add. Drew represented the new breed of policemen . . .

'Well, if you're asking me, I wouldn't mind the place as my country home.' Higgs braked to a halt. 'Always provided I wasn't expected to pay the bills.'

Jean opened the front door and asked them in, then left to call Poulton. Brice looked at the linenfold panelling, the suits of armour, the open fireplace that could swallow half a tree, 'the patterns of antique arms, the paintings, the refectory table with its lustrous patina, the silver, and the carpets, and was glad that such beauty could still be owned and appreciated.

Jean reappeared and led the way through to the library. Poulton remained seated.

'Good morning,' said Brice, in his quiet, slow, friendly voice. 'My name's Detective-Constable Brice. I think you've met PC Higgs before?'

Poulton nodded.

'I'm sorry to bother you like this, but the matter is important and you may be able to help us.' As an instructor sergeant had once said to Brice, sugar pulls the bees quicker than vinegar.

'I've given what help I can,' said Poulton shortly.

'That's true enough. Nevertheless, there are still one or two questions we'd like to ask.'

'Then you'd better bring over a couple of chairs and sit.'

Four matching leather-seated chairs were lined up by one of the bookcases and they carried two across and set them in front of the desk.

Brice said, 'Do you know Mr Michael Ansell?'

'He's the man who was first on the scene at the hit-and-run, isn't he? I've met him that once, yes, but only for a few seconds.'

'He received a threat over the telephone and then the night before last he was walking back to his house when a car very nearly ran him down. What we're trying to establish now is whether that was, in fact, an attempt to murder him.'

'So why come here?'

'Because what has happened to you may go some way to providing an answer . . . Did you, just over a week ago, receive a letter containing a thousand pounds in fifty-pound notes?'

'I've already answered that question. In fact, wasn't it you I spoke to?'

'You're quite right, it was. But I'm wondering whether, in the light of a possible attempt to murder Mr Ansell, you'd feel like reconsidering your answer?'

'I can reconsider it as often as you like, but it'll remain the same.'

'That amount was sent to Mr Ansell and it was

accompanied by a letter which made it perfectly clear the money was an attempt to bribe him into not giving us any more information.'

'So now you're asking me, by inference, whether a similar attempt was made to bribe me and, not being of such stern rectitude, I succumbed? It would be more gratifying if you'd assume that were I open to being bribed, it would take more than peanuts to close the position.'

'A lot of people would see a thousand pounds as a great deal more than peanuts.'

'I thought it was my actions and reactions and not anyone else's you were interested in?'

Brice thought for a moment, then said: 'Have you recently received a telephone call threatening you with violence if you don't keep silent about the hit-and-run?'

'I've previously answered that question as well.'

'If it was an attempt to kill Mr Ansell, you could be in danger now. And we can't really help you unless we know all the facts.'

'As far as I'm concerned, you do. And rest assured, I have a strongly developed sense of self-preservation.'

'Then you think you may need to call on this?'

'It's a shark-infested world and unless you want to be eaten you have to do that all the time.'

There was, decided Brice, little point in continuing the interview. He thanked Poulton and they left.

As Higgs settled behind the wheel of the police car, he said: 'He's a right cocky bastard!'

'Yes, he's that. And did you notice something else about him that's interesting?'

'Such as what?'

'There's a watchfulness about him which for my money says there's been a time when he's been worried that the police were getting too close for comfort; he's not always been as respectable as he makes out now.'

'He's rich, isn't he?'

'That's Alf talking, isn't it, not you?'

Higgs didn't answer. He liked Brice, even admired him, but there were times when he found him rather pious. He started the engine and drove off.

'If I'm right, then maybe it answers something that's been worrying me—why would a man in his position hang on to a thousand quid bribe? When he says that that sort of money is peanuts to him, he's telling the truth . . . If he was once on the other side of the fence, he kept that thousand because it gave him a belly laugh to be bribed for not telling us something he wouldn't have done anyway.'

'How's that again?' asked Higgs.

Brice smiled good-humouredly.

They reached the end of the drive, passed through the gateway, and then halted at the road to let a couple of cars pass.

'I'll tell you something.' Higgs drew out as soon as the second car had gone past. 'I'd have enjoyed our visit more if I could have had another look at his woman!'

Poulton looked in the telephone directory to find out how many Ansells were listed. Twelve. Four lived a long way from Ingleton, so it seemed sensible to check the remaining eight first. Each time, he introduced himself as a reporter on the *Stillington Gazette* who was following up the story of the hit-and-run and he asked if it was correct that Mr Ansell had actually witnessed the accident? The first four people didn't know what he was talking about, the fifth, a woman, sharply suggested he should speak to the police.

He wrote down the address of M. D. Ansell.

CHAPTER 12

An XJ-S had parked so that it was difficult to drive round its tail; Ansell cursed the driver as he reversed on opposite lock before once more going forward, a manœuvre which allowed him to complete his run into the garage.

As he entered the hall, he heard the murmur of voices from the sitting-room and he swore again. He was tired and would have far preferred not to have to be polite to a visitor ... He'd just hung up his mackintosh on the heavy mahogany stand when Brenda came out of the sitting-room, carefully closing the door behind her. She said, in a low voice: 'It's Stephen Poulton.'

After a moment he identified the name. 'What does he want?'

'I've tried to find out, but he keeps sidestepping an answer. Mike, he's perfectly pleasant, but there's something about him I just don't trust, and that's not because he didn't return to help the poor man on the bike ... Be careful.'

He nodded. She was a good judge of character, except where a reluctance to become too critical made her over-generous.

When he entered the sitting-room, Poulton came to his feet and shook hand. He asked if Poulton would like some coffee.

'Yes, I would, thanks.'

'I'll ask Brenda to make another cup.' He left and went through to the kitchen where Brenda was pouring coffee beans from a plastic container into a grinder. 'Make extra, will you? He'd like some.'

'It's all right, I was reckoning he would.'

He turned to leave.

'Mike, don't forget. Be like the deaf cobra.'

'What deaf cobra?'

'Which refuseth to hear the tune played by the charmer.'

'That one! I can never understand how, if it's deaf, it can be said to be refusing to hear the pipe.'

'Consult yourself for the answer.'

He returned to the sitting-room. 'Coffee won't be long. I don't smoke, but go ahead if you'd like to.' He sat. 'Have you heard any recent news on how the old boy is getting over his injuries?'

'Can't say I have.'

'He must have been badly shocked and at his age anything like that takes a long time to get over, doesn't it?'

'I suppose it does . . . I'm here because I reckoned it would pay to have a bit of a chat. You've been keeping in touch with the police, haven't you?'

'That's right.'

'You told 'em about receiving a thousand pounds through the post?'

'Of course.'

'Why d'you do that?'

'Because it seemed to me the money was intended as a bribe.'

'So?'

Ansell showed his astonishment. 'Then obviously I had to tell them about it.'

'Without stopping to consider the whys and the where-fores?'

'How d'you mean?'

'I don't want to be rude, but I'd say you haven't an idea about what's going on.'

Brenda, carrying a tray, came into the room. When she saw Ansell's expression, as he took the tray from her, she said: 'Is something the matter?'

'I'm not really certain.'

She looked uneasily at Poulton. Instinct told her that in

some as yet undefined way he presented a threat to her husband.

Ansell offered the tray to Poulton, then carried it over to an occasional table and served Brenda and himself. He spoke to Poulton. 'Perhaps you'd explain what you meant when you said just before Brenda came in that I'd no idea what was going on?'

'I'll try.' Poulton drank, put the cup and saucer down. 'Suppose I asked you if you thought a thousand pounds means much to the ordinary person, what would your answer be?'

'Very definitely, yes.'

'Then if the thousand you received was a bribe, it was a pretty big one?'

'That must follow.'

'Will you accept that no villain is ever going to offer a large bribe unless he's good reason, which means he's running a large job?'

'That sounds logical.'

'Right. Then this one's running a large job and so he's going to get very annoyed if anyone starts getting in his way. Now do you understand?'

'No, I'm afraid I don't.'

'You've obviously never had to look after yourself! . . . The other night someone tried to run you down, right?'

'Probably not.'

Poulton showed his surprise. 'That's what the police said to me.'

'I don't know what they said about it to you, but I told them that it probably wasn't deliberate.'

'If they believed you, why did they come asking if anyone had had a go at me?'

Brenda said, her voice sharp: 'For heaven's sake, Mr Poulton, why can't you explain what you're getting at straightforwardly instead of going round in circles?'

'All right. You, Mr Ansell, received a thousand quid in

the post. It was a bribe. A sensible man would have kept quiet about it, seeing it was doubly in his own interests to do so; a thousand falling out of the sky never hurt anyone and the reference to the three monkeys showed how to stay around long enough to enjoy spending it. Likewise, a sensible man wouldn't have gone running to the police to tell them about the threatening telephone call because the only effect of doing that would be more inquiries by the police and those further inquiries would tell the person who sent the bribe and made the threat that neither was doing any good.'

'I had to tell the police,' said Ansell forcefully.

'Why?'

'Without wanting to sound pompous, because it was my duty to do so.'

'Forget the window-dressing and concentrate on staying alive.'

'Forget what you call window-dressing and I call duty, and there'd be no law and order.'

'D'you want to stay around or don't you? Set yourself up as an example and you'll become an example to be avoided at all costs. Haven't you once thought out what can happen if you go on like you've started?'

'Not in the sense you seem to mean, no.'

'How can anyone be so careless?' he demanded rhetorically, appalled by such stupidity.

Ansell chose it as a question that required an answer. 'There's a principle involved.'

'And there's nothing so goddamn dangerous to everyone as a principle.'

'You don't believe in them?' asked Brenda.

'I learned to steer clear of them a long, long time ago. But because the world's a bloody unfair place and your husband is a great man for principles, I'm in the firing line. I do all the right things, like a sensible man does, but because the police inquiries continue I get a phone call saying my throat's in trouble if I go on talking . . . And I wasn't even given the chance of saying that the three monkeys haven't had a thing on me. Now it seems someone tried to run your husband into the ground. And still he goes on about principles!'

'The police are investigating,' said Ansell.

'Isn't that what I'm complaining about?'

'You don't understand that to give in to threats is to betray justice; betray justice and that's the end of all civilization. History proves that over and over again.'

'I understand something much more important. When you've had your throat cut, you don't care what happens to justice.' Poulton stood. 'It seems like I've had a wasted journey, but I'll try once more. The villain running this job won't care what he has to do to keep it moving. He started nice and easy, hoping we'd be sensible. When he found one of us wasn't—but unluckily for me, not which one of us— he got a little rough. If it still seems to him we're being soft, he'll become a whole world rougher.'

'If it becomes necessary, the police will protect us.'

'Like they protected you from that car? You know your trouble? You see the world as you want it to be, not as it is. But if you won't listen to reason, listen to some advice based on hard experience. Stop looking to the police to help you because when the chips are really down, the only people they're interested in saving are themselves.'

'That is very bad advice,' said Brenda.

Poulton shrugged his shoulders and left.

CHAPTER 13

The Devil's Dyke was a triangular cleft in the Downs due east of Stillington, said to have acquired its name from the time when the ashes of two witches burned at the stake had been thrown down it. From the top there was a view across a large tract of land to the sea and because of foreshortening the countryside seemed to be overwhelmingly wooded.

Dora Brice snuggled a little more deeply into the blanket she had wrapped around herself. There were times when she thought that she deserved a special place in heaven for having successfully concealed from her husband through all the years of their marriage the fact that she disliked picnics when a keen easterly wind was blowing, the sun spent most of its time behind clouds, and the ground was damp.

Brice stared out at the grey-blue line which marked the sea horizon. His eyesight was still good enough to pick out a couple of ships making their way down Channel, but for once his mind did not follow them to romantic places and he continued to ponder the problem of how to force Wright into a corner. To work his deception, Wright had had to dispose of two cars—the Granada involved in the hit-and-run and the second Granada which had been stolen to substitute for the first. A car was quite a difficult item to dispose of successfully, but one way was to send it to a demolition and recycling unit where it could be stripped and crushed into a small cube of unidentifiable metal. Knowing how closely they were watched by the police, such units were mainly honest, but a well-filled envelope often persuaded a small team to work late and forget. Every good detective would know which yard in his parish had employees who were susceptible to well-filled envelopes, so a request to all divisions in the county to make inquiries might well gain results . . .

Dearborn, tall, thin, and with a face so haggard that it suggested some slow disease, asked his foreman: 'What did the coppers want?'

'The usual. They're making inquiries about a couple of new dark blue Granadas. As I said to 'em, who's going to be such a bloody fool as to want a couple crushed?'

'Some of 'em are so dumb they have to think hard to remember their own names . . . What did they answer?'

'Seemed to think someone wanted 'em vanished. That's easy done, but for a profit, I told 'em. Slap on new numbers, give 'em fresh papers, and ship 'em over to the Continent.'

'I don't suppose the stupid bastards had ever thought of that!' Dearborn produced a pack of cigarettes and offered it.

Twenty-five minutes later, when satisfied he was unobserved, he left the yard and walked down the road to a call-box. It hadn't recently been vandalized and he was able to make a brief call and to pass on the news about the police inquiries.

In the master bedroom in Highwood Manor, Poulton listened to the field manager of the security company which had just completed the installation of an advanced electronic alarm system on the second floor.

'We've checked all circuits, Mr Poulton, and they're all go. To activate, simply press down the master switch.' He indicated the largest switch, painted red, on the control panel which had been set up on a three-foot-high stand to the side of the large double bed. 'And to de-activate, simply return the switch up.'

'How long will the batteries last?'

'Seventy-two hours of continuous running after mains electricity is cut. When the electricity is restored, they are automatically recharged and at full capacity after five hours.'

'And the alarm really can differentiate between me or Miss Rodgers moving about and anyone else?'

'That's right. The computer is programmed to recognize just you two, so if anyone else moves anywhere on this floor, the alarm will be triggered. It was to do the programming that we had to weigh and measure Miss Rodgers and couldn't just rely on the figures she gave us.' He coughed.

'In fact, hers proved to be significantly wrong. I hope the lady wasn't too upset?'

'I imagine that'll depend on how great and in which direction the differences were?'

The field manager smiled. 'The firm's motto is, Service with Confidence, so I hope you'll excuse me if I don't answer . . . You shouldn't have the slightest trouble, but if any problem does crop up, just get in touch with me and I'll be along right away to sort it out.'

'I'll do that.'

The field manager left, still wondering why a second, and very expensive, alarm system had been installed when the house had already been protected by a good one.

Poulton walked over to a window and looked out at the garden. He wondered if he were panicking and making a bit of a fool of himself. Was he really in danger because of the naïve stupidity of the Ansells, or was he allowing the threat far too much weight?

He went downstairs. Amanda had been watching the television, but the programme had been boring her—it was on the arts—and she switched the set off as he entered the room. She had used less make-up and her clothes were simpler than usual and there was about her an air of deceptive innocence. 'Steve, I could do with a drink.'

'So what's new?'

'Be a sweetie and give me one.'

He walked over to the mobile cocktail cabinet. 'Name your poison—gin, whisky, brandy, vodka, rum, Martini, Malibu . . .'

'Let's have some bubbly.'

She probably chose champagne, he thought, because she knew the Bollinger had cost over twenty pounds a bottle. He went through to the kitchen and then down to the cellar and brought up a bottle which he put in the ice bucket he'd bought the day after he'd read that a connoisseur never used a refrigerator to chill his champagne.

Back in the TV-room, once the breakfast-room, he filled two flutes and handed her one. She drank, then put the glass down on the arm of the chair and traced a pattern on the frosting with her forefinger. 'Steve, what's going on?'

'With reference to what?'

'Why have you had the alarms put in?'

'Why shouldn't I?'

'But the house was wired up before. You never do anything without a good reason, so are you expecting trouble?'

She was almost showing signs of intelligence, he thought. 'There are a lot of very valuable things around the place.'

'But most of them are downstairs and the new alarm is only for upstairs.'

'Who told you that?'

'The man in charge, after he insisted on weighing me. And he also said that the system already installed was one of the best of the ordinary ones.'

'He talks too bloody much for someone in security.'

'For heaven's sake, why shouldn't he talk to me?' She paused, then said, bitchily certain the question would annoy him: 'Who are you afraid of?'

'No one.'

She dipped her forefinger in the champagne and then ran the tip around the edge of the glass; after a while, a high-pitched note began to sound.

'How about changing the tune?' he said roughly.

'I'll change mine if you'll change yours.'

He suffered a sudden change of mood and said: 'So I'll show you mine if you'll show me yours.'

She had to giggle.

Brenda came to a stop in the middle of the landing and looked back. 'Did you remember to lock the kitchen door and bolt it?'

'I did,' replied Ansell, as he reached the head of the stairs.

'And the same with the front door?'

'Fear not. The drawbridge is up, the portcullis is down, and Castle Ansell is secure.'

She walked on into their bedroom, waited until he entered, and then said: 'Mike, are you sure you're taking things as seriously as you ought to?'

'Yes. It's just that I'm not going to spend all day and all night looking over my shoulder.'

'But quite apart from everything the detective said, Poulton did come here specifically to warn you.'

'To save his own skin . . . I thought you agreed with me, forget the gentleman—with apologies for the use of the word in such a connection.'

'Forget his stupid cynicism, of course, but not his warnings. He's in a much better position than you to evaluate the possible dangers.'

'Which is a polite way of saying you think he's a crook?'

'It certainly wouldn't surprise me . . . Mike, there was that car which so nearly ran you down.'

'I've told you, over and over again, I'm convinced it was just a drunk who probably never saw me and still doesn't know how close he came to killing someone.'

'Poulton wasn't convinced and he said the police couldn't be either because they were continuing to make inquiries.'

'You may be right, I may be right, but I can assure you of one thing. No one can possibly break into this house without making a great deal of noise and at the first sound I'll seize my trusted niblick.'

She said, angry because she was scared: 'What will be the good of that when you're such a lousy golfer?'

He tickled her and, as always, she had quickly to beg for mercy. She linked her fingers behind his neck and kissed him. 'Can't you understand that if anything should happen to you I just don't know what I'd do?'

'You'd soldier on, which is what one half of every marriage eventually has to do.'

'Then pray God that our "eventually" doesn't happen for years and years.'

'A very loud Amen to that.'

'Promise me one thing, Mike?'

'With you this close, I'll promise you a thousand and one.'

'If I go first, no bun-fight after the service. It's so difficult to decide whether people are mourning or celebrating.'

'If one's not around to be either gratified or insulted, I can't see that it matters . . . Now, for heaven's sake let's stop being so morbid.'

'I'm sorry, but I've a feeling that something awful's going to happen.'

'The last time you had one, you won a hundred pounds on the premium bonds; maybe this time things will be worse and you'll discover you've won a thousand.'

'Sometimes I could throw things at you.'

'You'd miss.'

They were professionals. They had studied a map of the countryside surrounding Highwood Manor and had noted the pattern of lanes, the copses large enough to provide cover, and the high ground to the north. They drove up to a vantage-point on the high ground and found, as expected, that from there they had a clear view of the house and grounds. Electricity came in from the south-east, along a line of wooden poles; the telephone from the south-west. The house was obviously well built and in a very good state of repair; it seemed certain there was double-glazing throughout; on the north side of one steeply pitched roof was a large skylight; on the back wall, midway between the first and second floors, was a square metal alarm box, painted bright yellow.

Camps, the older man, carefully focused the very high-power, twin-arm binoculars, of the kind used for artillery spotting, which were set on a tripod. He studied the alarm box. 'It's an Armadale,' he said firmly.

Unwin swore.

'So there's pressure pads, heat and movement sensors, reserve batteries in case of electricity failure, and like as not a direct line through to the nearest cop shop; could even be closed circuit telly.'

'What's he keeping, the Crown Jewels?'

'If he is, they stay there.'

'But why?'

Camps didn't bother to answer. He adjusted the binoculars until they were focused on the skylight and after a while he said: 'That's too obvious a break-in point; it'll be covered all ways.' He checked the windows on the first floor. 'They won't have sensors in the main bedrooms or corridors—someone needs a slash in the middle of the night, he's going to get up and walk and doesn't want the alarms telling everyone what he's doing . . . There's only the two of 'em living in and they'll have the best bedroom which'll face south. So we'll take one facing north . . . Give us the sextant.'

Unwin passed him a sextant and he used this to measure the angle between the windowsill of one of the first-floor rooms and the ground. The large-scale map they were using gave them the distance between themselves and the house and it was a simple calculation to work out the precise height of the windowsill.

CHAPTER 14

They passed through Stillington in a stolen van—it had been repainted a different colour and given new logos and registration number—at ten o'clock on Thursday night when there was still some traffic around so that there was no reason for their passage to be remembered. Camps drove and Unwin sat in the passenger seat; in the back, making themselves as comfortable as they could, were Susie and

McKenzie whose job it would be to remain in the van once it was parked in order to keep watch on the radios—Camps was obsessively security-minded—and (Camps also had a cruel sense of humour) to behave as a courting couple should there be the need to disarm suspicion.

The van drove off the road and into a copse on the north-east side of Highwood Manor and parked in a small natural clearing that was out of sight of the road. They waited, mostly in silence, three of them smoking heavily, until Camps decided it was time to move. He slid back the driving door and cool fresh air flowed in to replace the smoke.

They unloaded the van and then Susie and McKenzie settled in the seats. He switched on the two radios that were tuned to normal police frequencies and when satisfied they were working properly reported that fact to Camps.

'Let's move,' said Camps.

Unwin picked up some of the equipment, then spoke to the two in the cab. 'Don't do anything I wouldn't.' He was still sniggering when he followed Unwin along a narrow ride.

Slowed by the equipment, because of its unwieldy bulk rather than its weight, they continued through the copse to a barbed-wire and sheep-netting fence, which they climbed with the help of sacking. They crossed two fields—in the first of which snorting shapes almost unnerved Unwin who was not familiar with cows—to reach the hedge which marked the garden. Near this, on the south-east side, was the last of the electricity poles. Unwin strapped linesman's spurs to his boots, secured a pair of heavily insulated cutters to his belt, and then with the aid of a loop of rope climbed the wooden pole with all the ease of a South Sea islander ascending a palm. He cut through the wires. Now all house lights and TV cameras, if fitted, were out of operation; the alarm system, working on emergency batteries, remained operational.

They went round to the last telephone pole and Unwin ascended this and again cut the wires. If they were unlucky enough to make a mistake which set off the alarms, these would not now also sound at the police station, nor could anyone in the house dial 999.

They entered the garden through a gateway and crossed the lawn to a gravel path which bordered the north side of the house. They assembled three sections of lightweight aluminium ladder and with the foot set on the gravel, carefully raised it. Their calculations had been correct and the padded end came exactly up against a window-sill.

Camps checked ski-mask and gloves, then climbed the ladder carrying a canvas holdall in his left hand; he set this on the windowsill. The curtains were not drawn. From the holdall he produced a modified stethoscope and put the end of this against the glass; there were no sounds from within. This still left the possibility, however remote, that there was someone in the bedroom who slept silently with curtains undrawn. He used a torch, whose bowl had been painted over except for a small circle in the middle, to shine a very narrow beam of light inside the room. Detail was difficult to make out, but soon he was certain that the bed was empty and the door shut. Again using the torch, he checked the design of the double-glazing frames.

With a glass-cutter, he crisscrossed the glass of the central pane of the lower sash window. He squeezed the contents of a tube of glue on to the scored glass, pressed on to the glue a square of thick sacking. Then, mentally crossing his fingers for luck, he swung a hammer against the glass. It did not crack because the blow had not been sufficiently strong. Cursing himself for being so nervous, he swung again, harder, and the glass shattered, but only one small piece fell. He eased the sacking away and it brought with it much of the glass; he removed the remaining slivers by hand. That done, he checked the inside of the window frame and found alarm contacts which would operate if the window were raised more than three inches.

The double-glazing, set in aluminium framing, consisted of two halves which met in the middle of the window. With only a third of the outer sash window glass free, he did not have full access to either half of the double-glazing and so could not risk trying to break the glass as he had done before. This meant he had laboriously to drill a hole through the bottom framing so that a length of flexible wire, with a loop at the end, could be worked through to the inside.

Once the wire was inside, he had to loop it over the catch which fastened the two halves of the double-glazing. The task called for skill, endless patience, fingers that worked on through the pain of cramp, and a temper that did not explode when imminent success suddenly turned to failure. Eventually, he was successful. Once the loop of wire was over the catch it only needed a steady pull to force the catch back. He slid open one frame.

He descended the ladder with the holdall and left this on the ground. Unwin handed him the fourth section of ladder and he climbed back up and very carefully passed it through the window for its full length, then allowed the far end slowly to drop to the floor—pressure pads would be set only a little way back from the window, where a person climbing over the sill could be expected to put his feet; it had to be a possibility that these had been installed and had been left active in normally unoccupied bedrooms since there was a small chance of their being set off by mistake. As soon as Unwin had joined him and was ready to hold steady the outer end of the bridging section of ladder, he began to crawl along it, cursing the edges which, although rounded, dug deeply into his knees.

Poulton was awakened by the flashing light on the control panel by the side of the bed and it was in character that his first reaction was one of satisfaction—he'd proved himself to be smarter than the intruder. He switched on the bedside light, which did not work. So the intruder was a professional who had cut the electricity. He climbed out of bed, picked up a torch from the floor and switched it on, reached over to the control panel to switch on the small auxiliary light on it. The digital read-out said that the break-in point was in No. 12 room and a small handwritten list identified this as the third bedroom along the north side. The read-out said that now there were two intruders.

He lifted up the telephone receiver and was unsurprised to find that the line was dead. There was a rustle of bed-clothes and this reminded him that he had to alert Amanda to what was going on. He went round to her side of the bed, put his hand over her mouth, shook her and whispered: 'Keep absolutely quiet. Someone's broken in.' She began to shiver and she made a whimpering sound, like a puppy in fear.

He went over to the end built-in cupboard, whose left-hand door had been left open, and brought out a twelve-bore and a box of cartridges. He broke the gun and inserted two cartridges, closed the breech carefully to prevent any noise. He wedged two more cartridges between forefinger and middle finger, and middle finger and third finger, of his left hand, with the brass caps on the inside—this would allow him to re-load in a split second yet leave his hand free to hold the torch.

He returned to the control panel. The intruders had moved on; one was in the corridor and one was in bedroom 5. He watched, learning from their movements how they were operating. It was soon clear that one man checked a bedroom while the other remained in the corridor . . .

He moved as they reached the bedroom next but one to his. He'd sprayed the hinges of the door and it opened with only a whisper of sound, inaudible unless one were waiting for it. He stepped out into the corridor, torch ready, gun in his right hand. There were sounds which suggested the

second man had returned to the corridor. He switched on
the torch. The two men, looking grotesque because of the
ski-masks, were both caught in midstride; the leading one
lost his balance and staggered into the wall.

He made certain that the muzzles of the gun were clearly
visible in the torchlight. 'Lie down on the floor, on your
stomachs.'

The leading man regained his balance, but neither moved
to obey the order. Poulton guessed how their thoughts
were running—the ordinary householder might wave a gun
around, but he'd be far too soft ever to fire it. 'Nothing,' he
said forcefully, 'would give me greater pleasure than to have
a good excuse for pulling the triggers on two bastards who've
come to rough me up.'

They ceased to doubt his determination. They lay, face
downwards, on the carpeted floor.

'Amanda.' There was no answer and he thought he heard
her whimpering again. 'Get out of the bloody bed and put
something on and then come out here,' he ordered roughly.
After a moment, she looked round the doorjamb, one bare
shoulder visible, her face twisted with fear.

'Go downstairs and use the CB set to contact someone
and tell 'em to call the police.'

'Why don't you telephone?' she asked shrilly.

'Because they've cut the bloody wires.'

She disappeared, to reappear a minute later in sweater
and slacks. She sidled out of the bedroom, terrified by the
men on the floor.

'Have you got a torch?' he asked.

She shook her head.

'Then get the other one in the bedroom. The electricity's
been cut as well.' It was, he thought, like dealing with a
child.

She went back into the bedroom, returning with a torch
similar to the one he had. She hesitated, reluctant to leave
him, but when he gestured angrily she began to move along

the corridor, at first slowly, then with ever increasing speed so that by the time she reached the stairs she was almost running. Her one desire was to make the call and then rush back to his side and the safety he represented

Since Susie could be certain McKenzie would not make any demands on her, she had from the beginning been relaxed and friendly. They knew a number of people in common and she was recalling an amusing incident— amusing to everyone but the man involved—when a radio message came through which stopped her in mid-sentence.

'One Two to Bravo Oscar One Four. Proceed to High-wood Manor, East Blean, where a break-in has occurred and the owner is reported to be holding two intruders. I say again, proceed to Highwood Manor, East Blean, where a break-in has occurred and the owner is reported to be holding two intruders. Over.'

'Bravo Oscar One Four to One Two. Message received and understood. Am at junction of Orlon Street and London Road; proceeding to East Blean. Over.'

'Thank you, Bravo Oscar One Four. Message timed zero one one five. Over and out.'

Susie said, her voice shrill: 'We've got to get out of here fast.'

McKenzie picked up a walkie-talkie and repeatedly tried to call up the two men in the house, but there was no reply.

'For God's sake, let's go,' she cried.

He turned in the seat and reached over to pick up from the floor of the van a torch and an automatic. He slid open the door.

She stared at him. 'Christ! You're not going in, not with the coppers on their way?'

He climbed out of the cab.

'You're bleeding mad,' she shouted. He did not switch on the torch and almost immediately was lost to sight. She longed to drive off and escape, but knew that if she did so and McKenzie avoided being caught, he'd make certain that she bitterly regretted having done so. Not for the first time in her life, she cursed all men.

Poulton checked the time. It was now almost a quarter of an hour since Amanda had spoken over the CB radio to a truck-driver who'd promised to call the police.

She had been watching him from immediately inside the bedroom. 'How much longer are they going to be?' she asked, her voice shaking.

He was contemptuous of such fear . . .

She screamed as he saw a man, gun in hand, step out of a bedroom beyond the captives. He dropped to the ground, rolling the torch away from himself as he did so and it hit the wall and went out. A shot was fired and there was a blast of light and an explosion which hurt the eardrums; he'd no idea where the bullet went. He pulled the for'd trigger of the shotgun and because the butt hadn't been hard into his shoulder, the kick jolted him. There was a high-pitched scream. He fired again, broke the gun and the empty cases were ejected. He reloaded with the two cartridges he'd been holding between his fingers. There were sounds of frantic movement and he fired in their direction. A shot was fired back and this time he heard the bullet strike the wall to his left. Now he'd only one round immediately available and he waited, finger crooked round the after trigger; the only sounds were those of Amanda's sobbing.

He moved back, with the stealth of a foraging leopard, and his foot touched hers and she shrieked. But this produced no further shot. In a whisper he asked her for her torch and she abruptly held it out so that it prodded him in the side and almost caused him to fire for fear that he was being attacked. He took the torch and pushed her arm to direct her to move backwards and after a moment's hesitation, she did so. He knelt in the doorway, switched the torch on, holding it in his left hand at arm's length. The corridor was empty.

He went into the bedroom for more cartridges and re-loaded the right-hand barrel, then went over to the control panel. There were no longer any intruders in the house. He left despite her frantic pleas not to do so—and checked the north-facing bedroom by which they'd entered. A length of ladder lay on the floor and the window was open. He switched off the torch, crossed to the window, and felt the ladder outside; it was not vibrating to any movements.

He stared into the darkness, his thoughts bitter. He'd not been so bloody clever after all. He ought to have realized that professionals might well be smart enough to leave someone listening in to the police broadcasts . . .

He heard the sound of an approaching car that was being driven really fast. The police—late as usual, when they were really wanted.

CHAPTER 15

In the interview room, Brice wondered uncertainly what kind of a man Poulton really was behind that coolly smooth and at times arrogant exterior. He'd all but outguessed the mob who'd broken into his house, yet they'd obviously been real professionals; one of the shots could not have missed him by much, but it seemed he'd remained as cool as a cucumber . . .

Poulton turned over the last page of the thick volume of mug shots. 'He's not in this one.'

'Will you look through the next book, then?'

Poulton stared at the five remaining volumes on the table. 'A job for the day?'

'I'm sorry to say, there are quite a few more if these don't help.'

'I'm beginning to wonder if it's worth the effort.' But his expression belied his words. When those men had broken into his house, they had shown their contempt for him and his possessions and he would do anything in his power to punish them for their presumptuous stupidity. He continued his task, and as he turned over a page of the fourth volume he said with a satisfaction he did not try to hide: 'Here's the bastard!'

Brice stood and went round the table and looked down at the middle set of photographs which Poulton was indicating with a rigid forefinger. 'How certain can you be?'

'I never mistake a face.'

'Then we're in luck . . . That's number four-three-six-five.' He returned to where he'd been sitting and looked through several sheets of names until he found the identification he wanted.

'Who is he?'

'I'm afraid that for the moment it's confidential information.'

'But not for long, I hope!'

Cordington-on-Sea had once been a popular resort for the more prosperous holidaymakers, but with the postwar boom in incomes, leading to package tours for the millions, its fortunes had sharply waned; those who in the past would have gone there now preferred the Seychelles or Maui, not least because such places were still, in general, beyond the pockets of their hairdressers. The country club and the squash club were the first to vanish; the cinema tried showing Continental masterpieces (as films with sub-titles were described) and then skin flics before finally it too had to close; shops stocked poorer quality goods; and houses slowly gained the tatty appearance which was inevitable when the people no longer took any pride in living in them.

McKenzie and Gault lived in a house in East Cordington. McKenzie was heavily built, as strong as an ox, indifferent to other people's feelings, and quick to anger; Gault was slightly built, not very strong, intelligent, emotional, concerned with other people, and timid. Someone had once nicknamed them Beauty and the Beast, ignoring the fact that however deep the love, it seemed impossible McKenzie could ever be transmogrified into a handsome prince.

Brice, who'd been driving, pocketed the keys, put his hand on the door catch. 'Listen, Ernie,' said Drew, 'I reckon it would be best if you leave me to do all the talking.'

'How's that?'

'We want to crack this case quickly and McKenzie's one of the real hard bastards.'

'Yeah, I know.'

'So it's no good pussyfooting.'

'But . . .'

'Just leave everything to your Uncle Alfred.'

Brice shrugged his shoulders and wondered once again if Drew would ever learn that a head-on approach so often led only to a sore head. He opened the door, stepped out, and walked round the car to the pavement.

A six-foot-long path, which hadn't been weeded in years, led up to the front door. When Drew hammered the knocker with unnecessary force, a flake of green paint peeled off the door and fluttered to the ground.

The door was opened by Gault, who was dressed with care in a sweater and slacks; his hair was naturally curly and had been expertly styled.

'We want a word with Scotty,' said Drew, his tone contemptuous; even if he'd not previously know about Gault, he'd have identified him on sight as a catamite.

'I'm afraid he's out,' said Gault in his soft, warm voice which still retained a trace of Liverpudlian accent.

He'd just finished speaking when there was a shouted demand from inside to know who the caller was.

'I guess he must have returned when you weren't looking,' said Drew, as he pushed past and entered the house. The tiny hall was dismal and it smelled of damp. 'Is he in there?' There was only the one door—except for an opened one beyond which was the kitchen—and Drew turned the handle and went into the room.

There was too much furniture for the size of the room, most of it new; in one corner was a very large TV, video, and stacked music centre. There were a couple of empty beer cans in the grate and Gault hurried forward, picked them up, and dropped them into a waste-paper basket.

McKenzie had been drinking beer. He lowered the can and stared with hatred at the two detectives. His collarless shirt was stained down the front, his chin was heavily stubbled, and his small eyes were bloodshot. 'Why d'you let these bastards in?'

'I tried to stop them,' replied Gault nervously.

McKenzie drank again and emptied the can, threw it into the grate. He stared at Gault, daring him to retrieve it and put it in the waste-paper basket.

'You look as if you've had a heavy night,' said Drew. 'Where were you?'

'What's it to you?'

'We're interested because there's been a break-in at East Blean. Know the area, do you?'

'No.'

'Nice part of the country. Highwood Manor's a prime target and early this morning a couple of villains had a go. But the owner was smarter than them and he lined 'em up at the end of a shotgun. He wasn't quite smart enough, though, and he didn't reckon on a third villain, you, listening in on the radio and then turning up to rescue his two mates.'

'Not me.'

'I know it sounds very unlikely—you, risking yourself like that—but that's what the evidence says, so we've got to believe it.'

'What evidence?'

'Your big trouble was, you weren't very smooth and forgot to put on a ski-mask. So the owner of the house got a good look at your ugly mug and he's identified you.'

'Then he needs to get his bleeding eyes tested.'

'Not so. He's twenty-twenty vision.'

'Last night I was with mates.'

Gault spoke eagerly. 'I was with him all the time.'

'I'll bet!' said Drew contemptuously. 'So what were all you mates doing together, if that's not a rude question?'

'We were playing poker.'

'You wouldn't recognize three queens unless you saw 'em walking.'

'If you're so bloody smart,' shouted McKenzie, 'ask Terry, or Bob, or Shorty.'

'D'you mean Terry Ash, Bob Older, and Shorty Playford? I wouldn't believe 'em if they were wearing haloes when they told me the time.'

Playford was a small, nervous, quick-speaking man, with a wide, toothy smile and a butterfly desire to be pleasant; he effusively welcomed Drew and Brice into his house and three times tried to persuade them to have a drink before he finally accepted that they didn't want one. He answered their questions with every appearance of a desire to help them to the best of his ability. 'Of course I know Scotty and Adrian, Mr Drew; great people, even if there are those who talk a bit funny about Adrian—as I always say, it takes all sorts.'

'Yeah. Even ones like you.'

He laughed, to show a couple of gold-capped teeth.

'So when did you last see Scotty?'

'It's funny you should ask me that, seeing as I saw him and Adrian only last night. Except it was really this morning, but then one always talks about last night even when one means early this morning, doesn't one?'

'Count me out of anything you do.'

'You've a great sense of humour, Mr Drew. As I always say, it's that what distinguishes you lot from the coppers on the Continent. No sense of humour, them. Not that I ever try to get funny with the law wherever I am . . .'

'You try, but you don't succeed.'

'Mr Drew, I swear to you on the memory of my sainted mother that we were playing poker.'

'No respect even for your own mother? When are you trying to say that Scotty was with you?'

'All the time we was playing and that must have been from eleven to . . . maybe four this morning. I wanted to finish earlier because I was down a couple of centuries . . .'

'You'll be down a bloody sight more if you go on lying.'

'Mr Drew, may God turn me into a pillar of salt if I'm lying . . .' He paused, but nothing happened.

Ten minutes later, the two detectives returned to the car. Brice started the engine. 'I'm afraid that that didn't get us very far.'

'Are you saying you could have done any better?' asked Drew belligerently.

Brice shook his head as he engaged first and accelerated away. But he had been commenting on the case, not denying the possibility, and the same thought nagged at him later as he sat at his desk and stared into space. How in the hell were they ever going to get anywhere? When equipment had been abandoned on a job, it usually afforded valuable clues, but here it seemed it would not. No fingerprints, all identifying marks removed or erased; the make of sectional ladder was a popular one, with too many units sold for there to be a reasonable chance of tracing these; the torch, glue, cardboard, and glass-cutter could have been bought from almost anywhere; the two bullets had shattered; footprints in the flowerbeds were not even good enough for casts to be taken; tyre marks in a nearby copse identified the size of tyre, but it was one which was used by several models of cars and light vans; Poulton identified McKenzie, but McKenzie had an alibi which for the moment just couldn't be broken . . .

CHAPTER 16

Ansell arrived back from work and parked the car in the garage. He unlocked the front door and stepped into the hall. 'Brenda.'

She called out: 'I'm upstairs, checking the laundry.'

'Is everything all right?'

'Yes.' She appeared on the landing. 'Why d'you ask?'

'Well, you weren't in the hall.' He realized how absurd that might sound to anyone else. After twenty-five years of marriage, he was still perturbed if she was not waiting to kiss him hullo.

But there was no third person present and she was gratified that he needed the reassurance. 'I'll be down in a second to make the coffee.'

'I'll put the kettle on.' He went through to the kitchen and half-filled the kettle from the tap, then plugged it in. He wandered over to the window and looked out and realized that the back lawn needed mowing. He'd do it tomorrow, he decided. *Mañana.* The Spaniards' greatest gift to civilization.

Brenda came into the kitchen and kissed him warmly. 'Well, what kind of an afternoon have you had?'

'Very typical. When it wasn't frustrating, it was fatuous.'

'Come on, it can't have been that bad.'

'Far, far worse.'

'Now tell me what's given you such a bad case of the glooms? Have you been indulging in too many if-onlys?'

He looked at her, surprised she should have divined his thoughts so correctly.

'Remember, if ifs and ands were pots and pans, there'd be no work for tinkers' hands.'

'How I hate that saying! It's so smugly self-righteous. And far worse, it denies me my daydreams.'

'You feel frustrated?'

'Very.'

She smiled. 'Something tells me that you've just moved from one subject to another . . . Before I forget, Inspector Bream rang earlier.'

'He sounds a bit fishy.'

'God, Mike, you don't improve! . . . He's the local crime prevention officer and would like to have a chat with us. I said to be here around six-thirty.'

Inspector Bream was a dapper man who had an earnest way of speaking and who lowered his voice slightly whenever he wished to make a point. When asked if he'd like a drink, he explained that normally he never drank on duty, but that it was the exceptions which proved the rules.

He raised his glass of lager. 'The first today and thrice welcome for that!' He drank. 'Your wife will have told you, Mr Ansell, that I'm the local crime prevention officer. It was DC Brice who suggested I come along and have a talk.'

'Has something more happened, then?'

'You haven't seen the local news on the telly?'

'No, I haven't.' He looked at Brenda and she shook her head.

'In the early hours of this morning, two men broke into the home of Mr Poulton.'

'Good God!'

'Luckily he had prepared himself for just such an event and he caught the two men and called the police. Unfortunately, however, before we could reach his house, an accomplice turned up and managed to free them.'

'What were they after?'

'The house contains a lot of valuable things, but to be

frank we don't believe burglary was the real motive. It seems more likely that it was their intention to assault Mr Poulton.'

'Then that car *was* trying to kill Mike,' said Brenda.

'I don't think that that follows because, as I understand things, there's a strong possibility that the driver was drunk.'

'You've nothing to prove he was, have you?'

'No, Mrs Ansell. But then neither have we anything to prove that he was sober and intending murder.'

'I'm sure it was just a case of drunken driving,' said Ansell.

Her voice was sharp. 'I've told you before, Mike, for God's sake stop trying to protect me from the truth.'

'The truth, Mrs Ansell,' said Bream, 'is that although we can't be certain, on balance we do not believe that there was an attempt on Mr Ansell's life.'

'All right, let's leave it there. But your coming here now must mean that because of what's happened to Mr Poulton, you think there's likely to be an attack on my husband.'

'I'd put it like this. There has to be the possibility that there will be an attempt to persuade your husband not to cooperate any further with us. And that's why I've come along—to advise you on how to make certain that any such attempt fails.

'The most obvious answer is for both of you to move out of here, leaving nothing to suggest where you've gone. We can make certain that things like the forwarding of mail give nothing away.'

'For how long would this have to go on?' asked Ansell.

'Impossible to answer, since we don't yet know why it's so essential to someone that you and Mr Poulton refuse to help the police identify and prosecute the driver of the hit-and-run car.'

There was a short silence, broken when Ansell said: 'It's not easy to think of somewhere where we could stay. A hotel is out of the question because of the cost and as for friends, my grandfather always used to say that guests were like fish, they began to go off after three days.'

'Don't you have any relatives who might be a little more ... well, hard of smelling?'

'There's my brother-in-law, but he lives in Shropshire; obviously, I couldn't commute from there.'

Brenda said: 'You wouldn't have to. You tell the company what the trouble is and they'll understand.'

'They'd understand and express their sympathy, but they'd also distance themselves from my problems and say that if I want to keep my job I have to turn up and work. And who could blame 'em? What firm these days is going to hold a job open for anyone for an indefinite period? ... But there's certainly nothing to stop you going up and staying with George.'

'I wouldn't do that on my own.'

'As I've just said, I can't go.'

'Then that's that.'

Ansell turned to Bream. 'Wouldn't it be best if my wife left here?'

'It would have to be safer, Mr Ansell. And there's another point; if she did, you wouldn't have to worry about her safety.'

She spoke forcefully. 'If you're staying, Mike, so am I.'

'But that's being stupid.'

'Then I intend to be stupid.'

Bream was a tactful man. 'Perhaps it would be best to look at the problem from a different angle. How well is this house protected from illegal entry?'

Ansell said: 'Pretty well, I'd judge.'

'Then all outer doors can be bolted as well as locked and they all have chains on them?'

'Both front and back doors have bolts, but in fact only the front one has a chain.'

'What about windows—do they all have security catches?'

'The downstairs ones do, but not the upstairs ones.'

'Is there an alarm system?'

'No.'

'Then to begin with, I think you should have one installed immediately.'

'How much is that likely to cost?'

'The kind I would like to see you put in would work out at between two and two and a half thousand pounds.'

Ansell whistled.

'I am talking about the latest state-of-the-art. It's that which tripped up the villains who broke into Mr Poulton's place.'

'Would there be a grant to help pay for the installation?'

'I'm afraid not.'

Brenda said: 'In order to protect ourselves properly we need to install it, but if we can't afford the cost, that's our bad luck? The State, which after all is supposed to do the protecting, couldn't care less?'

'No, Mrs Ansell, that's not how things really are. After all, I'm here as a representative of the State and I'm doing all I can to help.'

'By suggesting something that's too expensive for us?'

'I'm talking about what is best. Naturally, a system not so elaborate will cost considerably less.'

'And offer less protection?'

'I'm afraid that has to be true, yes.'

'So the richer we are, the more protection we can enjoy?'

'It's no different from any other aspect of life,' said Ansell, worried that Bream might be feeling embarrassed. 'The rich fly Concorde, the rest of us sit cramped up in an ageing 727.' He turned to Bream. 'How much would a more mundane system cost?'

'One that could be considered adequate? Roughly seven hundred and fifty pounds.'

'Then we'll just have to settle for one of those.'

'I'll give you a list of local firms who can undertake the

job and whose work has proved to be good—I strongly suggest you contact one of them. Then in addition to that, I think you must put a chain on the back door and catches on the upstairs windows. Do you have a telephone in your bedroom?'

'We've only the one receiver and that's downstairs.'

'Then it would be a very good idea either to get a cordless one or to have an extension fitted . . . Would you like me to have a word with British Telecom and ask them to make it a priority job?'

'Which should ensure that we have the extension by the beginning of next year?'

The Inspector smiled. 'I'd hope to be able to persuade them to move a whole lot more smartly than that . . . I believe DC Brice mentioned to you about not becoming isolated from other people when you're out?'

'He did, yes.'

'Try and keep that in mind all the time, won't you? . . . I'd like to have a look around the house, if I may, to see if there are any more suggestions I can make, but just before that I do want to make something very clear. We will be doing everything we can to support you. You'll know that it's our policy now to get our chaps out of cars and back on the beat—whoever's on this beat will have instructions to keep a very close eye on this house. Also, patrol and panda cars will be told to make a turn around the close whenever that's possible. Villains are usually deterred when they see that somewhere is under special police watch.'

Poulton left the Jaguar and crossed to the front door. Once inside, he was immediately aware of an unusual silence— there was no music being played too loudly—and he called out Amanda's name. There was no reply. Gone shopping, he told himself; after all, it was at least a couple of days since she had bought herself any clothes.

He went through to the TV room and poured himself a

whisky and soda and thought about the air tickets he'd just collected. The two first-class flights to Zürich, where a suite at the Baur au Lac was booked. He'd a little business to deal with, then they'd fly on to somewhere warm and sunny, where there'd be no risk of anyone calling unannounced at one in the morning. He welcomed a holiday, but still cursed Ansell for being such a naïve fool that it was necessary to take one right now.

He went upstairs to change and found the bedroom was in an unusual state of disarray; the top of the dressing-table was in confusion and doors of two of the cupboards had been left open. He went over to the cupboards. There were few clothes left on the hangers and all drawers had been emptied except for odd garments which had been discarded. He turned and checked the bed. The furry bear, in which she kept her nightdress, was not on top of the bedcover.

Behind one of the mezzotint prints depicting scenes from ancient Rome was a small combination safe. A couple of months ago he'd had reason to wonder if she'd learned the combination; when he opened the safe and found that two thousand pounds in cash were missing, he realized that she had.

He knew a growing anger, fuelled not so much by the loss of the money as by the knowledge that she had left him before he had decided to get rid of her.

CHAPTER 17

Ansell, who was sitting up in bed, cleared his throat.

'No,' said Brenda, 'I will not.'

'You've no idea what I was going to say.'

'Dear man, when you sit there looking like Moses finding the golden calf, it's obvious you're thinking momentous thoughts. You're wondering how to persuade me to go and stay with George for a while.'

'The Inspector did say you ought . . .'

'I don't give a damn what he said.'

'But you'd be safe with George.'

'Let's get something straight. I am not going to let some nasty little swine separate me from you. For heaven's sake, normally you'd be the first to say that in the name of freedom one has to refuse to be intimidated.'

'I know, but . . .' He became silent.

'But this is different because the principle isn't painlessly abstract, it's painfully immediate?'

'It . . . Well, it does make a difference when it's someone one loves.'

'I imagine all high-minded principles become very different the moment one is actually involved in them. My trouble is, I don't care about principles, I care about people; and I listen to my heart, not my mind, and that tells me that I share your life whatever happens.'

He wished that she loved him less and herself more.

Police held informers in contempt but, being realists, worked with them since without their help, far fewer cases would reach the courts. Higgs made a U-turn and parked the car near to a street light which wasn't working, half way along the road which ran directly above the pebble beach. He wound down the window and the light wind, spicy with the tang of the sea, ruffled his hair. Well out to sea a ship, showing two white masthead lights and green sidelight, was almost abeam. When he'd been young, he'd often thought of going to sea . . . He saw Rainer approach and he wondered with the arrogance of youth how any man could allow himself to lose so much self-respect.

''Evenin', Guv,' said Rainer, in his hoarse voice which correctly suggested years of drinking the cheapest available spirits. 'You're keen on Scotty? Him and Bert Camps've been doing business lately.'

'D'you know what they've been up to?'

'Only that they've been working together.'

Valuable news, or worthless? Higgs didn't have the experience to judge.

Camps lived in Trentstone, four miles from Cordington-on-Sea in distance, but four hundred in character. Throughout the years it had been a seaside town which unashamedly catered for people who wanted jellied eels, a ride on the dodgems, a knees-up on the Victorian pier, and pubs which welcomed sing-songs. Whereas Cordington had declined and decayed, Trentstone had continued to prosper.

Camps's house was a semi-detached in a road of semi-detacheds, all built to the same design but now to some extent individualized by a variety of home improvements. Ada, referred to in courts as his common-law wife, was a big, strong, harsh-tongued woman who was fiercely loyal. 'What d'you want?' she demanded.

'To have a chat with him,' replied Drew.

'What about?'

'I can tell him that when I see him.'

She looked at him and Higgs with open hatred. 'Can't ever bloody leave a man alone, can you?'

'Not when he keeps as busy as Bert does.'

'He's been going straight for years.'

'Then maybe you ought to tell him that, so as he knows.'

She realized that there was little to be gained by continuing to be obstructive and contemptuously said they could enter.

They had less than a minute to wait in the front room—comfortable, slightly untidy, a place in which to put up one's feet and watch the telly—before Camps, followed by Ada, entered.

Drew stared at Camps's right arm which was in a sling. 'Been in the wars, have you?'

Camps sat on the settee, Ada remained standing, thick arms crossed in front of her generous bosom.

'Come on,' said Drew, 'let's have the news.'

'What's it to you?'

'Quite a lot, if you're suffering from a gunshot wound.'

'Get stuffed.'

'Now that's not a very nice way to talk on a Sunday . . . You might as well tell us now. Or we can ask around—hospitals, doctors, quacks—and find out who treated you and it won't look good, you denying everything.'

'I was out on the mud.'

'That must have made you feel at home.'

'I was after duck and some stupid bastard tried for a low-flying one and hit me instead.'

'What makes you so confident it was a mistake? . . . I wonder if by any strange chance all this happened during Thursday night?'

'It was the morning flight on Friday. We'd been playing poker . . .'

'Hold on, don't rush things—you're really interesting me. Who was rash enough to risk playing poker with you?'

'Jim, Scotty, that little queer of his, Terry, Bob, and Lefty.'

'I wonder who was cheating who . . . Scotty gave us the same load of crap, only he never mentioned you and Unwin. Now I wonder why not? Lack of imagination? Embarrassment? . . . Let's talk a bit more about the shooting on the mud flats. What happened?'

'I've just bleeding told you.'

'You reckon the next gun loosed off at a duck that must have been flying on its knees and hit you instead . . . A three-year-old could better that. I'll tell you exactly where you were when you were hit. In one of the upstairs corridors in Highwood Manor.'

'Give over.'

'Scotty's handed us the full story.'

'Then run the dumb bastard in for perjury.'

'Where were the pellets removed?'

'The general hospital.'

'Then we'll go along and claim them and have 'em compared with pellets from cartridges from the same box as Poulton was using.'

'They gave them to me as a keepsake on account of a few inches to the right and I'd've needed measuring.'

'Then you can give them to me.'

'I've thrown 'em.'

'What a pity Poulton didn't shoot a little to his left.'

Mumford sat on the edge of his desk and looked across at Brice. 'The old man's calling for an up-to-date report on the hit-and-run and subsequent events.'

'There's not much to report except failure.'

'He'll really like that.'

Brice sighed.

'Come on, give me something.'

'Look, Sarge, you know as well as me, there's nothing. After the break-in at Highwood Manor, Poulton identified Scotty McKenzie from a mug shot and nothing'll shake him, but Scotty has an alibi which so far we can't begin to challenge.'

'Then we're naming Camps, Unwin, and McKenzie, yet can't prove the involvement of a single one of them. Can we be wrong?'

'No.'

'It's easy to say that and then shut up, but I'm going to have to give the old man reasons. And how do I do that when so far we haven't even established a definite connection between the various incidents, let alone gained any idea of what they all add up to?'

'The sequence is too exact for us to be wrong; the bribe was followed by a threat, which was followed by action— the pressure was increased each time it became clear our investigations hadn't been halted. That proves we're right.'

'If I try to say that that proves anything, the old man will read me his lecture on fitting the conclusion to the facts, not the facts to the conclusion.'

'He can be difficult sometimes.'

'Not sometimes, always . . . And do you know what he's going to be most difficult over? If he agrees the events probably are connected, even if we can't prove it, he'll ask what it's all about. What do I say to him? That we haven't an earthly and are waiting for inspiration?'

'As a matter of fact, Sarge, I've been thinking. You'll remember that the Granada was going down Ingleton Hill, which means it was travelling north, or away from the sea? There's still a fair bit of smuggling goes on, so suppose Wright had picked up a cargo and couldn't afford to be caught with it?'

'Having got clear of the accident, he'd almost a week in which to get shot of the cargo before we identified him as the driver. Once he was shot of it, he'd nothing to worry about except getting pinched for bad driving and not stopping after the accident. He's not going to hire a top-class mob to do some strong-arm work on the witnesses when a good lawyer, at a tithe of the cost, could convince the average jury the skid was bad luck and in the misty conditions he didn't realize he'd hit the old man.'

'Which means the cargo must have been something that couldn't be moved immediately and leaves him at risk even now. So what is it? Drugs? They could have been shifted that night and the same goes for every other cargo except one; somebody who couldn't be moved on easily because of the risk of him being recognized. Don't forget, Poulton said there was a passenger in the Granada.'

'All right, let's look at the idea. Who could fit the bill?'

'One of the villains who's been sunning himself on the Costa del Crime and now needs to do a spot of business over here; an IRA hit man . . . You can draw up a list as long as your arm. All we can say for certain is that he's likely to be recognized, if only by the likes of us, and once recognized, his reason for being here will be obvious.'

Mumford looked curiously at Brice, surprised he was showing so much more imagination than usual.

Brice spoke urgently. 'We need a search warrant for Wright's place.'

'Not a hope on what little evidence in support we can produce.'

'But we've got to try and prevent a tragedy.'

'You know as well as I do that we can only work according to the book.'

'And provided we do, it doesn't matter what happens to the Ansells?'

'We've done what we can for them. Didn't Inspector Bream go to their place and advise on security?'

'Yes.'

'And he suggested they leave for a while, but they refused? That puts the ball in their court.'

'For God's sake, Sarge, it's just not that simple. He can't leave the area because of his job and she won't go if he won't.'

'Then there's nothing more we can do.'

'At least you could suggest to the old man that we make inquiries along the coast to find out if anyone saw something on the day of the hit-and-run that could give us a lead.'

'All right, I'll do that, but with the pressure of work at the moment, it may be difficult to get him to agree to it.'

'Make him understand.'

'One doesn't *make* him do anything.' Mumford slid off the desk and went round it to sit in his chair. 'Poulton's proved himself a tough nut to crack; what kind of a man is Ansell?'

'About as different as you can get.'

'Are you saying he won't be any good at looking after himself?'

'In a straight scrap, I suppose he'd be as useful as the next man. But if they go after him it won't be a straight scrap and he can't seem to realize that. He thinks that the fact he leads an honest life protects him from any villainy.'

'More fool him.'

'But forty years ago . . .'

'It's not forty years ago, it's now.'

'Yeah . . . Sarge, instead of just keeping an eye on his house, couldn't we run a continuous watch?'

'Impossible.'

'Why?'

'A continuous watch ties up a minimum of eight blokes in twenty-four hours, what with reliefs, illnesses, court appearances, and all the other things which keep a copper from his proper job.'

'What if it does?'

'Now you're just talking daft. If eight men are tied up looking after someone who's been advised to clear out and has chosen to ignore that advice, then those eight aren't there to help people who haven't been given any chance to escape.'

'You just won't understand. Can't you see that Ansell could be terribly badly beaten up . . .'

'Suppose you learn one thing. You haven't a bloody monopoly on caring what happens to other people.'

'I wasn't trying to say I have, but . . .'

'From my side of the desk it sounds like that's precisely what you're claiming.'

According to the job demands, thought Brice with a sense of bitter frustration, Mumford was acting with perfect correctness.

CHAPTER 18

They were professionals. Therefore they could judge that because the close was horseshoe-shaped, their job was going to be both easier and more difficult. With only one entrance, movement was restricted, but from inside No. 7 surveillance of the outside would be simpler; the presence of a strange man or vehicle was more likely to be observed, but any police presence was easier to pick out . . .

They stole a light van, changed the number plates, colour, and logos (removals expertly executed—they were not without a sense of black humour), drilled two observation holes in the side, and parked this just beyond the entrance to the close at a point from which they had a good view of No. 7.

The observer saw that workmen were fitting an alarm box on the side wall. After the work was finished, he used a small terrestrial telescope, sighted through the larger observation hole, to check the box visually. The system being installed was not of a very sophisticated nature.

Later, a patrol car turned into the close and drove slowly around, then left without stopping. The police were keeping an intermittent and not a continuous watch on the place, noted the man in the van.

The uniform PC climbed the five wooden steps up to the coastguard hut and entered, grateful to escape the cold wind which was blowing in from sea. ''Afternoon, Tom.'

'Hullo, there!' said Badger cheerfully, glad of the company. 'Not seen you in a month of Sundays, so where've you been hiding?'

'We've a new inspector and he reckons there are twenty-five hours in every day.'

'Give him time and he'll learn . . . Feel like a cup of char?'

'You don't need to ask twice.'

As Badger put the kettle on the ring and lit the gas, the PC said: 'I'm here to ask if you noticed anything unusual on the twenty-first of last month—a Monday.'

'I'll check in half a minute.' He prepared the teapot and then went over to where the log was kept. He turned back the pages until he came to the day he wanted, read the entries. 'The only thing that happened was a call from Reg, over at Murchley. He wanted me to keep an eye on a motor-cruiser that had just cleared harbour.'

'What was his interest?'

'He didn't say for certain—plays things close to his chest, does Reg. But visibility was bad and the ordinary fair-weather sailor would've stayed in harbour, so he reckoned the boat was worth watching. Or maybe he'd had a tip-off.'

'Did you see the boat?'

'Some time later I checked the radar and there were two small craft ten miles out, slowly converging—one of 'em could've been Reg's boat. The two blips came together for a bit, but the radar doesn't have good resolution at that range so it didn't mean they ever definitely got closer than about two hundred yards.'

'They didn't stop?'

'There was no time to transfer cargo, no.'

'Not if that cargo was a man?'

Badger scratched his chin. 'If he crossed in a small inflatable, the boats would have kept sailing and I wouldn't have noticed anything on the screen.'

'Do you know the name of the boat you were asked to watch out for?'

'I seem to remember Reg mentioning it, but since the two boats didn't heave to, I didn't bother to note it in the log.' The kettle began to boil and he returned to the gas ring, poured a little water into the teapot to warm it, emptied the water into the sink, and measured out three spoonfuls of tea. 'There's one thing, mate; you get a proper cuppa served here.'

Thirty minutes later, the PC parked outside Alldyke's house in West Murchley. Alldyke, somewhat pompously, said that he'd a good memory and didn't need to check the books; the boat's name was *Cistine III* and she was on charter through Steerly and Long. As far as he'd been concerned, there'd been no reason to pursue any inquiries concerning her.

Steerly and Long were boat-builders as well as yacht brokers and their offices were on the west side of one of two large, ancient, and rather ramshackle sheds. A middle-aged woman, short and dumpy, listened to the PC's request and then checked the files. 'That's right, she was on charter on the twenty-first.'

'Was that just for the day?'

'Good heavens, no! With a boat like *Cistine III*, the minimum charter is for a fortnight.'

'When did this hiring start?'

'Four days earlier, on the seventeenth, and she was chartered by Mr Wright.' She emphasized her words to try to make it clear that a boat was always feminine and one did not hire, one chartered.

'D'you know anything about him?'

'Not really. We asked for references, of course, and he gave them, but these were really only concerned with financial matters.'

'Did he mention where he was sailing to?'

'I've a note that he said he might cross to France if the weather was fine. I confirmed that the insurance was in order for going foreign.'

The PC finished writing in his notebook. 'That seems to be everything. Thanks.'

She said, worried: 'Are we likely to be involved in any sort of trouble?'

'I couldn't really say. In a case like this, where we get a

request from another division to make inquiries, we're given some of the details but never enough to know what's really going on.'

Drew parked in front of Highwood Manor, left the car, and crossed to the front door. He knocked. When Jean opened the front door, he said: 'I'd like a word with Mr Poulton.'

'He's not here.'

'D'you have any idea when he'll be back?'

'Not really. He's gone abroad to find some sun.'

The rich weren't different, they just led different lives. 'Can you let me have his address?'

She shook her head. 'He's not going to let me know where to forward the mail until he's decided where to stay.'

'That's that, then . . . I suppose his girlfriend's gone with him?'

'She has not. She left him, because of the terrible time when those men broke into here.' Her tone suggested a certain moral satisfaction at the course events had taken.

As he returned to the car, he indulged in the tantalizing daydream of walking along the street and by chance meeting her . . .

There was heavy cloud, which was a good omen, and on the journey down to Stillington the three men joked a lot. But the jokes died away as they turned off the Stillington by-pass on to a road that took them round to the south side of the town.

They parked on rough ground, out of sight of the road. They crossed a triangular-shaped field, moving very care-fully because compacted molehills had made the ground uneven, to reach the four-foot-high post-and-rail fence which protected the back gardens of Nos. 4, 5, 6, 7, 8, and 9.

Once in the garden of No. 7, they split up; one of them went round the side of the house until he had a good view of the close, the other two carried on to the back door and after a quick check began the laborious task of boring a circle of holes in the middle of the wood. When this was completed, one of them used a keyhole saw, its blade frequently sprayed with silicone floor polish to prevent noise, to cut from hole to hole; just before the last section of wood was sawn, plastic tape was attached to the middle of the circle of wood to prevent its falling inside.

A metal rod, on which were fixed a mirror and a torch, was carefully inserted inside and by carefully moving the rod it was possible in the mirror to make out the new plaster in the wall, the bolts at top and bottom of the door, the chain, and the lock, as each was in turn illuminated by the torch. There was an angled clip near the end of the rod and the elder man fixed this to the door so that the torch was pointing at the new plaster. 'Give us the arms and compass.'

The extending arms, similar to those used by many disabled persons, had been modified to meet some more unusual requirements. The compass was gripped in the tong-ends and then inserted and the arms manœuvred until the compass was up against the new plaster; the needle moved, showing that at least one of the hidden wires was live, indicating a closed-circuit alarm system. He swore silently. It was going to be a long and finicky job. Had they been able to cut the incoming electricity wires, they might well have found that the alarm system operated on mains electricity only, but they dared not work at the front of the house because there was no way of judging when the police would enter the close.

It took him, and he was an artist at the work, almost fifty minutes to scrape away the new plaster and expose the two sets of wires, check that one was not carrying current which indicated an open circuit and so one that could be cut immediately, and to cross-contact the second circuit.

Again using the arms, he withdrew the top bolt and the chain and then, after adding an extension, the lower bolt. Probably because of all the other defences, the original lock had not been replaced and it took him less than a minute to force it with a tool that looked like an over-large dentist's probe.

He opened the door. Immediately inside the kitchen was a mat. Pressure pads were normally only activated by weight, so he carefully lifted the mat—no pressure pad. He shone the beam of a shaded torch across the floor. At a point where a person would tread who was deliberately stepping over the mat was a length of coir matting. He lifted this and underneath was the pad for which he'd been searching. One last test had to be made before they could move freely. He pushed a small meter as far as possible into the room; the needle did not flick, showing that there was no heat/movement-seeking unit in the kitchen.

They were crossing the floor when the bleeper sounded. They froze. Growing tension made them sweat. They imagined a police car driving into the close and the occupants noticing . . . The pager bleeped again to signify the all-clear.

They stopped at the doorway into the hall. Where, wondered the elder man, would he place a heat/movement sensor so that it operated most effectively? The answer seemed obvious. At the head of the stairs where it must pick up the approach of anyone climbing them. Switching on the meter, he used the extending arms to hold this out into the hall. At first the needle was motionless and it remained so until he'd taken four paces, then it began to flick. He studied the landing, which led off to the right from the head of the stairs and was open for a distance of some eight feet. They were in luck. Judging by the meter, provided they kept at least six feet to the right of an imaginary line from the side of the stairs, they should be OK. He turned and whispered: 'Ladder.'

Four minutes later he was handed a short, lightweight ladder. Carrying this in a horizontal position—awkward rather than difficult—and hugging the right-hand wall, he crossed to a point where he could set the ladder to reach up to the landing.

He climbed until he could reach over the banisters and, with the arms, check for pressure pads under the landing carpet. There was none. He signalled to his companion to call in the third man from outside.

CHAPTER 19

Ansell was dreaming that he was on the moors, searching for something the identity of which was confusingly uncertain, when he abruptly awoke to find that a light was playing on his face. He heard movements. His mind instinctively tried to block, insisting that his senses were playing him false and he was dreaming that he had awoken.

Brenda turned over. 'What's the matter?' she asked in a sleep-thick voice. 'Why've you put the light on?'

A gloved hand holding a leather cosh momentarily came into view as the torch was moved until the beam was focused midway between himself and her. There had been nothing dreamlike about the cosh.

The telephone was on his side of the bed, some two feet away, and it was a button one so that he could punch 999 as quickly as his finger could move. But even so, could the call possibly get through quick enough? . . . Not long ago —except that now it seemed a lifetime ago—he'd joked to her about relying on his trusted niblick; as soon as possible afterwards he'd searched for and found a length of wood that would act as a club and he'd hidden this in one of the cupboards so that she shouldn't realize that he was taking the threats more seriously than his words suggested. The cupboard was eight feet away, beyond the torch. The window was to his left, five feet from the edge of the bed . . .

'Mike, what is it?' The beam of the torch moved again to

concentrate on her. This woke her fully and she opened her eyes and after a moment's incomprehension realized that it was not a bedside or overhead light which was shining. She reached out with her left hand and felt that he still lay in bed beside her . . . 'Oh my God!' She moved her hand again, searching for his and when she found it, gripped it tightly.

The man who held the torch said in a strangely and disturbingly flat voice: 'Seems like you're a stupid mug. Don't know what's good for you.'

Ansell judged from the sounds that there were three men in the room. In the face of such odds, a direct attempt to escape or to call for help must almost certainly fail, so he'd have to rely on guile. Somehow, he had to fool them long enough to act. But to do what? There was small point in trying to reach the club; only a gun would have evened up the odds sufficiently. So did he try to distract them long enough to dial 999 and have the call answered? But how long was long enough? Surely more time than he could reasonably hope to gain. That left only the window. To the right of it was a chair and if he grabbed that and swung, he could smash both double-glazing and the window. The noise would be considerable and there must surely be a good chance it would alert someone in one of the other houses; or a policeman might be in the close, checking that all was well at No. 7. Instinctively, he believed that there must be a rescue. The cavalry always arrived in the nick of time . . . How did he distract their attention long enough to enable him to reach the chair? By making them think he was trying to escape by the door . . .

The man spoke again. 'And seeing you're such a mug, you've got to be taught.'

He decided to appear totally cowed. 'I . . . I . . .' He swallowed repeatedly.

'You . . . you . . .' said another man, and in sharp contrast to that of the man with the torch his voice was filled with mocking contempt.

'Please don't hurt me,' he cried. He tightened his grip on Brenda's hand, loosened it, tightened it again, trying to tell her that he was not really panicking. She showed she understood by repeating the pattern. He gently released his hand.

'All right, move,' said the man with the torch.

Ansell acted as if the command had been directed at him. He threw back the bedclothes, rolled over, and reached out for the floor with his feet; as he straightened up, he faced the doorway. Then, instead of charging forward, he thrust himself sideways with all the force he could muster . . .

A blow to the base of his neck stripped his limbs of all strength and he collapsed backwards, to land on the bed; there was an inner light in his head that was also a wildly growing pain. A second blow, this time higher up, caused him momentarily to lose consciousness. When he returned to his senses, a gag was being forced into his mouth and this was secured with a bond drawn so tight that his cheeks and mouth were distorted. It seemed as if the gag were slowly slipping down his throat to choke him and frantically he tried to hold it back with his tongue. He was rolled over on to his stomach and his arms were secured behind his back, with his elbows painfully drawn tightly together. Then he was turned face upwards once more.

Brenda began to plead with them, begging them not to hurt him.

'He's got to learn,' said the man with the torch.

Frantic, she thew herself on top of Ansell to try to protect him from the beating-up that they both believed was about to happen.

'Look at 'em, having a quick bang,' sniggered the third man.

'Belt up and get on with it.'

Two of them stepped closer to the bed and as they moved to drag her off Ansell parts of them appeared within the range of the torchlight and then disappeared. She screamed and with brutal efficiency and speed they thrust a gag into her mouth and secured it. She began to thrash about with her legs and one of them gripped her ankles.

'She's looking good, ain't she?'

Her nightdress had ridden well up her thighs and even at such a moment, instinctive modesty made her reach down to lower it. Her hand was knocked aside. 'Don't go and spoil our fun.'

A fear, far greater than that which he'd known when he'd believed their intention was to beat him up, exploded in Ansell's mind.

The man who was not holding her ankles grabbed hold of the hem of her nightdress and, exerting considerable strength, ripped it; he then tore the nightdress right up and threw the halves apart.

'She's got nice tits.'

'Too floppy for me, mate; I like 'em stiff.'

'I can show you something that's stiff.'

In Ansell's mind, he cried wildly on God, the Devil, or anyone else who could help. A pair of gloved hands reached out and fingered her body and he closed his eyes, unable to suffer further.

'Keep watching, so as you learn what happens to stupid mugs.'

Fingers dug into his neck and an intense pain, which unbelievably grew more intense with every second, taught him that there was nothing a man would not do to escape pain and he opened his eyes. His neck was released.

One of the men had a large white vibrator in his right hand and he switched it on; the low hum sounded like working bees. 'Ready for the fun, lady?' His lascivious tone made it obvious how much he was enjoying this. He inserted the vibrator. He was handed another, smaller one. He inserted that.

'Listen to her loving it!'

She was making a sound that only a perverted mind could have suggested denoted pleasure.

'So let's give her the real thing and then listen.'

'That's enough,' said the man behind the torch.

'Let's do the job proper . . .'

'Get 'em out.'

For a moment it seemed as if their lust had become too great for them to obey the order, but then one of them removed one vibrator and allowed the other to run free.

The torch was brought closer to Ansell's face. 'Listen, mug, that's just for starters. Keep on being stupid and it won't be just vibrators get shoved up next time—and afterwards, she won't be going nowhere.' The speaker's voice remained devoid of tone; unlike the other two, he seemed to have been unaffected by what had happened.

The three men left, briefly visible as black shadows. Brenda was still moaning and Ansell knew a wild, impotent, torturing self-contempt.

CHAPTER 20

The telephone awoke Brice. His movements automatic, he reached out and picked up the receiver.

The duty detective-constable said: 'Three men broke into Ansell's place, without setting off the alarms, and worked both of 'em over. Get down to the general hospital and question them as soon as they're up to it.'

He struggled to clear his mind of all sleep. 'How bad are they?'

'He received blows to the head and it's not yet known what the damage is; she was sexually assaulted, but not raped.'

He cursed, said he was moving right away, and cut the connection.

'What's the matter?' mumbled Dora.

'Sorry, luv, I've got to move.' He switched on the bedside light, climbed out on to the floor and went over to the chair on which were his clothes. 'I'll be a long time, so don't expect me back soon. There's a couple we needed to protect and we've failed.' He did up the buttons of his shirt. 'We bloody failed them,' he shouted wildly.

The doctor looked as tired as he felt. 'We're going to carry out one more test, but at the moment it looks as if he's escaped serious injury.'

'And Mrs Ansell?' asked Brice.

'Physically, her injuries are slight; merely some bruising.'

'And mentally?'

'She's suffered severely.' He ran his fingers through his hair that was already beginning to thin. 'They set out to humiliate her. God almighty, what kind of men can do such things.'

'Animals,' replied Brice hoarsely.

'Animals don't humiliate for pleasure.'

'I'd like a word with them as soon as that's feasible.'

'They both need to be left in peace.'

'But if I'm to learn anything that'll help to catch the bastards, I need to learn it fast.'

The doctor sighed. 'All right. I'll let you know when it's possible . . . Do you know them at all?'

'I've met them once or twice.'

'Can you say what kind of a woman she is?'

'The very best.'

'What I'm asking is, how strong a character is she?'

Brice searched for words that would accurately describe her as he saw her. 'She maybe seems gentle when things are smooth, but I reckon she'll fight tooth and nail if she has to.'

'She's going to need all the fight she can find if she's to get back to normal quickly.'

Brice wanted to smash something.

The doctor left and Brice sat in one of the chairs. He remembered the time that Dora had unaccountably been ill after the birth of their second son and he'd waited in hospital, terrified each white-clad figure was about to approach him and say she'd just died . . .

A nurse woke him up and his mind was so muzzy that she had to repeat her question before he understood her. 'Are you the detective who's waiting to speak to Mr or Mrs Ansell?'

'That's right.' He came to his feet.

'You can see Mrs Ansell now; but only for a moment.'

'How is she?'

'D'you know what happened?'

'Yes.'

'Then you can imagine . . . Look, do you have to see her now? Can't you leave it for a while?'

'If she knows anything that'll help us, the sooner she tells us the more chance we'll have of grabbing the men who assaulted her.'

'All right. But take it easy.'

'Of course.'

'And if she doesn't want to tell you something, leave it. She maybe won't find it so easy talking to you since you're not a doctor.'

They walked down two corridors and into a small room in which were two beds, only one of which was occupied. Brenda had been given a pair of pyjamas and a dressing-gown from the hospital's store of emergency clothing and both were too large for her so that she looked as if she'd shrunk slightly. A WPC had been sitting on a chair beyond the foot of the second bed and she came across and said in a low voice: 'We've been chatting because she wanted to. I don't think you're going to get much.'

'Maybe she'll remember something fresh.'

She hesitated, then returned to the chair. The nurse

remained by the doorway, he went over to the bed. 'I'm terribly sorry, Mrs Ansell,' he said, all too conscious of the inadequacy of his words.

She looked up at him. 'It's not your fault. The inspector advised me to leave the house, but I wouldn't.'

She should never have had to make the choice. Both the law and the police had failed her, yet by the rules they had acted perfectly correctly. The law demanded legal proof before action was taken in order to protect the innocent, but in the present liberal times this principle had been extended until it was the innocent who suffered. It was a humane principle that it was better ten guilty men went free than that one innocent man be found guilty. Better for that innocent man, of course, but what about the equally innocent people who suffered because the nine guilty men committed further crimes? The police had to furnish the legal proof of what they claimed before they could act, so that the innocent might be protected. But now that the law was biased in favour of the guilty, more and more innocent suffered. In many cases the police were rightly convinced of the guilt of a suspect, but that suspect was never charged because the police could not find sufficient legally admissible proof of guilt. If the police had been granted a warrant to search Wright's house, it was possible that enough evidence would have been uncovered to arrest him; then the foul attack on Mrs Ansell might never have taken place . . .

She interrupted his troubled thoughts. 'Won't you sit down?'

There was another chair by the side of her bed and he sat. 'Mrs Ansell, I'm terribly sorry to have to bother you like this, but I do need to find out how much you can tell me.'

'Yes, of course.' She spoke with quiet calm; only the way she continually plucked at the hem of the top sheet suggested an inner tension.

'Will you describe all you can remember, right from the beginning. Even the smallest detail could be enough to help us identify the villains.'

'But there's so little I can tell you. I was woken up suddenly . . .' As she described what had happened, the rate at which she plucked at the sheet increased.

'Did you ever see any part of their faces?' he asked.

'No. They were wearing knitted garments over their heads —ski-masks, I think they're called.'

'Did any of them ever remove his gloves?'

'No.'

'When they were leaving and you saw them as shadowy outlines, did you notice anything unusual about the way any of them walked?'

'No. But by then . . . Well, I wasn't noticing much.'

He saw the look the nurse gave him and knew that the interview was about to be closed. He said quickly: 'You think you heard each of the three speak; did any of them have a regional accent or use unusual words?'

She shook her head. 'All I really remember is the man with the torch. There was no tone to his voice and the way he spoke it was as if . . . as if it was all something ordinary and rather boring.' She gulped.

He stood. He thanked Brenda, tried and failed to find words of consolation, nodded at the WPC, and left.

Two hours later, he was allowed to question Ansell, but his evidence was of no more use than his wife's had been.

Brice left the hospital as the cloudless eastern sky was beginning to lighten. Already there were cars on the roads and a few pedestrians were hurrying along the pavements. Not for the first time in his career, he cursed because no matter how great a tragedy an individual suffered, the world continued just the same and that made all suffering meaningless.

*

Because she had been released from hospital before Ansell, Brenda was able to drive to the hospital to collect him. He was waiting in the main reception area and as she gripped his hand and reached up to kiss him on the cheek, she felt him begin to pull away, then stop. 'How are you, my darling?' she asked.

'Not too bad. But you?'

'No aches or pains.'

They left by the main doorway and went round to the car park and their Fiesta. She handed him the keys and he unlocked the passenger door and held it open for her, then walked round the bonnet to his door. As he settled behind the wheel, she said: 'It's almost lunch-time and I wondered if you would like to eat at Luigi's?'

'Would you mind very much if we went straight back?'

'Of course not.'

They reached home and he garaged the car, then joined her in the sitting-room. She waited for him to speak, but he said nothing as he stood by the settee, his expression both bitter and embarrassed.

'Mike, will you give me a really strong whisky—I feel I need it.'

He poured out the drinks and handed her one glass, then did not sit beside her on the settee as she so plainly wanted, but went over to one of the armchairs.

She said, trying not to sound too worried: 'What's the matter? You've hardly spoken a word since I picked you up at the hospital.'

'My head's begun to ache.'

'Is that the truth?'

'Yes.'

'Just before we were married, we promised to tell each other the whole truth if challenged. Is that the whole truth?'

He said angrily: 'For God's sake, what's the use of quoting what happened when . . .'

He stopped.

'When the world was a cleaner place?'

'Cut that out.'

'I won't. If we're to survive, we've got to tell each other the whole truth so that we can learn to live with it. Why are you acting as you are? Is it because of the filthy things those men did to me and now you can only see me as unclean?'

'Of course it isn't,' he said violently.

'Then why?'

He gestured with his hand, picked up the glass and drained it. 'Leave it.'

'I won't. Why?' she demanded again.

'Because . . . because I just watched what was happening and didn't do anything to help you.'

She left the settee and crossed to the chair in which he sat. She took his head and held it against herself. 'You tried, even though you knew it was hopeless; even though they might have killed you for trying. Never again, ever, begin to think that you let me down.'

He wished her passionate words could begin to wash away his sense of guilt.

CHAPTER 21

Mumford was seated behind his desk. He watched Brice cross the floor, then said: 'How are they?'

'How d'you think?'

'I don't know and that's why I'm asking.'

'The injuries to his head will heal fairly soon and there shouldn't be any permanent damage.'

'And the wife?'

'Christ, Sarge, do I have to spell it out to you how she must be feeling?'

Mumford fiddled with a pencil. 'Why d'you think the villains acted as they did?'

'Isn't it obvious? They humiliated the two of them because a humiliated person is so much more easily scared. And by not raping her, she's left with something worse to fear—a threat's only good all the time the victim's facing something worse than he's already suffered.'

Mumford put the pencil down. 'I hope this has taught you something, Ernie?'

'Like what? That there's no limit to man's beastiality?'

'That when a policeman starts thinking he's cleverer than the system, or he's morally superior to the rules, he's liable to hurt people. Have you thought that if you'd done as I said at the beginning and put the case on ice, the Ansells wouldn't have suffered?'

Brice said hoarsely: 'You don't mind putting the boot in, do you? All right, I'll give you something to bloody think on. If you'd agreed to apply for a search warrant for Wright's place, the case could have been wrapped up. So you're just as responsible as I am.'

'There has never been enough evidence to support such an application.'

'You can hide behind that smokescreen? You can really assure yourself that what happened to the two of them doesn't concern you, because you faithfully followed the rules? You can sleep easy?'

Mumford's face had gone white, as it always did when he was angry. 'I can sleep all right; but if I were you I'd find it goddamn difficult . . . Now get out and question Camps and find out if he was one of the three who broke into Ansell's house.'

Brice parked as close to Camps's house as was possible.

'D'you think he was one of 'em?' asked Higgs.

'I don't know.'

Higgs took a deep breath. 'D'you mind if I say something?' He spoke uncertainly.

'Depends what it is, doesn't it?' Brice replied.

'Alf was saying that you're . . . Well, he said you're too soft for the job because you're always worrying about what happens to people. But I reckon you're right and he's wrong.'

Brice turned and looked at the youthful, eager face and realized for the first time that Higgs was in some ways very similar to the person he had been many years before. He shook his head. 'Alf's right.' He saw that his answer had confused Higgs, but made no effort to explain it. 'Come on, let's find out if we've one of 'em lined up.'

They left the car and walked along to the house. Ada opened the door and stared at them with hatred.

'We'd like a word with Bert.'

'He ain't around.'

'When will he be?'

'I don't bleeding well know.'

'Look,' said Brice, and despite all his bitterness and anger, he still spoke pleasantly, 'we've got to talk to him, so unless you want us camping here you'd best tell us where to find him.'

'At the hospital, that's where.'

'What's happened?'

'Got smashed up by a drunken driver.' Just for a moment, her hard, aggressive attitude failed to conceal her deep worry.

'I'm sorry to hear that,' said Brice automatically. 'When was this?'

'Two days ago. Driving along and a drunken bastard comes out of a side road and straight into him and Jim.'

'Is that Jim Unwin?'

'What if it was?'

'How is he?'

'Might lose a leg,' she replied indifferently, concerned only with the injuries to Camps.

Brice thanked her and hoped that Camps would soon recover. She was still shouting abuse at him as he led the way back to the car.

'D'you reckon that's right?' asked Higgs, as he clipped the seat-belt.

'She's telling the truth, yeah. But we'll still go to the hospital now to make certain.'

'So he wasn't in on the Ansell break in.'

Brice started the engine.

Detective-Inspector Redstart-Havers had a quiet, polite manner, but there was no mistaking this for softness. He had his eyes on really high office and would always be prepared to use his feet as energetically as the next man to climb up there. His office was large enough to have appeared bleak had he not decorated it with several of his possessions, the most noticeable of which were two of his oil paintings which hung on one wall and which excited the secret derision of several of his subordinates. He said to Mumford, who with Brice stood in front of the desk: 'Is Camps warm?'

Mumford looked at Brice, who answered. 'Completely cold, sir. Both he and Unwin were in hospital at the time of the break-in.'

'Blast!' He opened a drawer and brought out a pipe and tobacco pouch. 'Has Wright been questioned yet about the motor-boat he hired?'

Mumford said: 'Someone's twice been along to the house, but there's been no one at home.'

He began to fill the bowl of the pipe. 'I want this case cracked. Make certain Wright's questioned as soon as possible. Are there any other leads?'

'Not at the moment.'

'Then you better pull your finger out and find some.' He tamped down the tobacco, struck a match, and lit the pipe.

When Ansell returned from a walk, he heard the sounds of a bath being drawn. Yet Brenda had had one earlier on. He crossed to the stairs, hesitated, then turned, shoulders slumped. Twenty baths a day would never wash away her memories. Just as twenty drinks a day would never drown his tormenting thoughts.

When she came downstairs, he was half way through his third whisky. 'Hullo, sweet,' she said. 'You're looking tired. I hope you didn't go too far? The hospital did say to take life easily for several days.'

'I'm all right.'

'I hope you really are.' She went over to an armchair and sat. 'Is this a private drinking session or can anyone join in?'

He poured out a ginger and whisky and had just handed her the glass when the front doorbell sounded. He went through and opened the front door to find that the caller was Brice.

'I hope this is a reasonable time to have a word, Mr Ansell?'

'I suppose it's no more unreasonable than any other time would be.'

Brice entered and after closing the door, Ansell led the way into the sitting-room. He noted how uneasy Brice was as he said that he hoped Brenda was feeling better. They'd become like the disabled, a source of embarrassment.

Brice chose a gin and tonic and it was some five minutes after his arrival that he said: 'The reason for coming here now is to ask you once again to run through all that happened.'

'Why?' demanded Ansell. 'We've already told you everything we can.'

'The thing is that people, especially when they've been badly shocked, often don't at first remember every detail of what they saw and heard, so after a while we get them to go over things again and then quite often they can tell us something fresh that's important.'

'We can repeat the facts a dozen times and it won't make any difference. They were hardly more than shadows.'

'I do know all that, Mr Ansell, but even so you might recall something which could prove to be of importance.'

'We'll help in whatever way we can,' said Brenda.

He thanked her. 'Before the break-in, did either of you notice a car or van hanging about the place? Or did you see anyone who doesn't live in the close . . .'

At the conclusion, Ansell said: 'Have you learned anything fresh?'

'I'm afraid not.'

'Then you're never going to identify and arrest the men, are you?'

'It's really much too early to say that. Any investigation takes time.'

'But you've had all the time since they broke into Poulton's house and you've got nowhere.'

'That's not right because it wasn't the same men.'

'I thought you knew nothing about them, so how can you be so certain?'

'As yet, we have no idea about the identities of the men who broke into this house, but we can be reasonably certain that we can identify the ones who broke into Highwood Manor. We've naturally checked those three and two of them were in hospital on Wednesday night and the third one is muscle, not brains, and in any case he had an equally solid alibi.'

'If you know that much, why haven't you arrested them for breaking into Highwood Manor?'

'Unfortunately, we don't have sufficient proof for arrest.'

'Not even though they abandoned a lot of equipment?'

'They were professionals—no fingerprints and all identifying marks removed.'

'Surely one of the maxims of police detection is that every contact leaves a trace? There must be traces on their clothes?'

'We need a stronger proof of involvement before we can take away clothes for examination.'

'God almighty! You believe in making life easy for them.'

'Not us, Mr Ansell, the legislators who make the law. And in any case, a smart criminal destroys all the clothes he wears on the job so that they can't be tested for traces.'

'Did you ever get as far as questioning them?'

'Of course. They all had alibis.'

'Which, if you're right, had to be faked. Presumably you can't prove that?'

'I'm afraid that's the way it is.'

'Could they have planned what happened to us, even if they didn't carry it out?'

'It's very unlikely. They're a team who are only smart enough when they're working to detailed instructions.'

'You're saying that someone gave the orders—have you any idea who?'

After a moment's hesitation, Brice nodded.

'And he'll have paid the three to break in here?'

'Yes.'

'Is it the man who was driving the hit-and-run car?'

'Probably.'

'How much of this did you know before Wednesday?'

'Quite a lot.'

'Why didn't you arrest him?'

'We lacked, and still lack, the necessary legal proof.'

'You could have put pressure on him until you gained that proof.'

'Mr Ansell, you're a lawyer so you must know we can't do that sort of thing.'

'All I know is, if you'd arrested him, my wife wouldn't . . . Who the hell is the law supposed to defend, the innocent or the guilty?'

They were in bed and something made her turn and look at him; it was obvious that although he had an open book in front of him, he was not reading. 'Mike . . . I want to snug.'

After a brief hesitation, he laid his book down and then put his arms around her as she moved across to him. She waited for him to respond to her advance, but when he did not, she said: 'Put your hand here.' He did not move. 'Why won't you make love to me? Because you think I'm unclean?'

'God, no!'

'Then why?'

'Because . . . because I failed you.'

'I've told you, again and again, you didn't . . . Make love to me, Mike, and we'll kill the past.'

Twenty minutes later, he muttered: 'I'm sorry.'

She held his head against her breasts. 'It doesn't matter.' But she knew that for both of them it did.

CHAPTER 22

Drew knocked on the front door of Wright's house; it soon became clear that once again there would be no answer. How many abortive visits had now been made? And like as not, Wright was sunning himself on some Caribbean beach . . .

A man, a fork in one hand, came round the side of the house. 'D'you want something, mate?'

'Me? I do this sort of thing for kicks,' replied Drew, with heavy sarcasm. 'Local CID. Have you any idea where Mr Wright is?'

'Can't say as I have.' The gardener pushed back his cap in order to scratch his head. 'Which is odd, seeing as it's pay day and he didn't say nothing about not being here to pay me.'

Drew's manner sharpened. 'Does he usually tell you if he won't be around on pay day?'

'Always has done—and given me the money early.'

'Are his cars in the garage?'

'One of 'em won't be, seeing as it was pinched and the insurance company, like always, isn't in a rush to pay up.'

'Let's go and see if the other's there.'

They walked round to the double garage on the far side of the house. The up-and-over doors were normally activated by remote control, but they could be hand operated and were not locked. The garage was empty.

The gardener scratched his head again. 'Must've gone off.'

'But you've no idea where?'

'He never said nothing to me.'

Ansell entered the front room at divisional HQ and asked to speak to Brice. After a ten-minute wait, during which he aimlessly leafed through some old police magazines, Brice came through a doorway and across the oblong room.

After a brief greeting, Ansell said: 'I want to ask you something.'

'Sure. The best thing is if we go through and find a free interview room. We won't be disturbed there.'

The first of the rooms was free and they sat on either side of the wooden table. Ansell asked: 'Have you got any further since yesterday? Have you learned anything that'll help crack the alibis of the men who broke into Poulton's house or nail the driver of the hit-and-run car?'

'I don't think so.'

'Don't you even know that much?'

Brice looked briefly at Ansell and was unsurprised to note the signs of stress. 'I suppose I was being over-cautious. You see, it's just possible that the results of the most recent inquiries haven't had time to reach me yet; but I can't honestly suggest that that's at all likely.'

Ansell spoke even more urgently. 'Then something's got to be done.'

'I promise you that we really are doing—'

'I read an article in a magazine which said that a larger proportion of crimes was solved through information received than as a result of actual detection work. Is that right?'

'I doubt very much that the proportion is larger; nevertheless, it is considerable.'

'Why does someone inform?'

'There can be any number of reasons, I suppose, but the main ones are revenge, jealousy, or money.'

'What sort of money is one talking about?'

'That's impossible to answer. Sometimes it's only enough for cigarettes and one wonders why the nark is really doing it, sometimes it's thousands of pounds, like an insurance company paying a percentage of the total value when whatever was stolen is recovered.'

'You said yesterday that the third man connected with the break-ins at Poulton's place was muscle and not brain —does that mean that he's simple?'

'No. It's just that Scotty's very much better at doing than thinking what to do. He'll never set up even a simple job on his own initiative, but carefully explain what's wanted and he'll do it, whatever the odds.'

'Does he live in Stillington?'

'No.'

'Then where?'

Perturbed by the intensity of Ansell's emotions, Brice replied without thought. 'In Cordington with his boyfriend.'

'What's his surname?'

Abruptly, Brice remembered the need to distance himself from emotion. 'Why are you asking that, Mr Ansell?'

'I've decided to offer him money to tell the truth.'

'I'm afraid it's very unlikely that'll work. He's a man with a strong sense of loyalty as you can judge from the way he went to the rescue of the other two at Highwood Manor instead of scarpering, as a hell of a lot of his kind would have done.'

'Even if the reward's a large one? Every man has his price.'

'I'd have thought you'd be the first to refute the truth of that.'

'What's his surname?'

'I'm sorry, but that information's confidential.'

'You don't think that after failing to protect my wife from those animals, you owe me at least enough to tell me?'

'No one could be sorrier than I am about what happened, but I cannot break the rules and give you the information.'

'They've broken all the rules—of decency.'

'I know, but . . .' He didn't finish.

'Yesterday, you virtually admitted that you've not been getting anywhere.'

Brice could argue no further because his sympathies were all with Ansell. 'I'll tell you what I certainly am allowed to do. You decide how much you can afford to offer and I'll see that word gets immediately to the detective chief superintendent at county HQ. He'll certainly agree to circulate a notice of the reward where it's likely to do the most good.'

'You make it sound as if no matter what's happened, everything must still go through the proper channels?'

'I'm afraid there's always a set routine.'

'Except for the victim.'

Ansell walked over to the window of the sitting-room and looked out. 'Brenda . . .' He stopped.

When he remained silent, she said: 'What is it?' She had not missed the note of strained tension in his voice.

'Will you do something for me?'

'If I can.'

'Go and stay with George.'

'Will I do what?' Her tone was suddenly antagonistic.

He was surprised by her reaction, but did not immediately interpret the reason for it. 'Go and stay with your brother in Shropshire for a while?'

'Can't you bear to have me around any longer?'

He turned and stared at her in amazement. 'For God's sake, why on earth ask that?'

'Isn't it obvious?'

'No, it isn't.'

'You find it difficult to admit you want me out of the way?'

'It's only so that there's no fear of your being hurt again. What did you . . .?' Belatedly, he realized the course of her thoughts. He crossed the room and gripped her tightly. 'It's me I'm having all the difficulty in living with, not you. But that's not why I'm asking you to go away. It's because I'm going to do something which may alert the bastards to the fact that I haven't listened to their threats.'

Her sense of worry and resentment became fear. 'You can't!'

'I must.'

'Why?'

'Because if I don't do something more I'll have let their threats gag me and that'll make me the coward that even if you say I'm not . . .' He shrugged his shoulders.

She longed to tell him that it was insane to worry about whether or not it appeared that the threats had had their desired effect, but she kept silent because she understood that he had to give himself the chance to overcome his self-contempt, however unwarranted such self-contempt might seem to anyone else. 'Mike, first please tell me what it is you're thinking of doing.'

'I'm going to identify one of the men who broke into Highwood Manor and then—'

She broke in. 'But how can you begin to do that?'

'The detective-constable may inadvertently have given me just enough information.'

She silently cursed Brice. 'What can you do even if you succeed in finding him?'

'Offer him enough money to persuade him to tell me who gave the orders.'

'Surely it should be the police who do that?'

'He's not going to admit anything to the police if to do so means they'll turn round and arrest him. But if he tells me, I can promise him that no one will ever know he did.'

She knew a small measure of relief because his proposed course of action was far less drastic than she had instinctively feared.

He said pleadingly: 'So will you go and stay with George?'

'When do you want me to?'

'As soon as you possibly can. Ring him up now.'

'But . . .'

'Please.'

'All right,' she agreed reluctantly.

He left Stillington station, having seen Brenda on to the London train, and drove on to the ring road which, a mile and a half later, gave access to the Cordington-on-Sea road. The countryside was rolling, with a typical patchwork of small fields, hedges, and copses, but for once he was indifferent to the beauty around him. How much would he have to offer before he could persuade the as yet unknown man to talk? Earlier, he'd drawn cash on his Access card and almost emptied their building society account and in his pocket was fifteen hundred pounds. Yet would it prove enough? He would, he told himself grimly, soon find out . . .

He reached Cordington-on-Sea as it began to grow dark and parked outside the first pub he came to. His plan of action was a simple one, perhaps because no other had occurred to him. He intended to visit each pub in the area and to say to whoever was behind the bar that he was looking for a friend of his whom he knew only as Scotty, a bit of a character who lived with a boyfriend . . .

The barman and the barmaid in the first two pubs seemed reluctant to answer freely and it was only as he was returning to his car the second time that he realized the reason for this. Initially, it convinced him that it would be much better (at least for his self-esteem) if he dropped the information about Scotty living with his boyfriend, but then he realized it would be stupid to do that because it was an important part of the identification . . . The correctness of this decision was shown at the third pub, the Cock and Four Hens.

The barman had long, wavy hair, carefully styled, a thin, artistic face, and manicured nails; he wore brightly coloured clothes and an art nouveau ear-ring in his right ear. He frowned as if something about Ansell puzzled and bothered him. 'You say the name's Scotty. But you don't know what his friend's called?'

'I'm afraid not.'

'Is he a big bloke, really strong?'

'That's right.' Ansell remembered Brice's description. 'And I believe he's been in a spot of trouble.'

'Happens to the best of us, so they say.' There was a call for drinks from further down the bar and he moved away. When he came back, he leaned his elbows on the bar. 'There's a Scotty who comes in here fairly regular and he's as strong as an ox and they say he's been in a spot of trouble in the past.' His tone became critical. 'Doesn't go much on shaving.' He paused, then added: 'His friend's name is Adrian.'

'Do you know his surname?'

'He's always just called Scotty, but I think I did hear . . . Now, what was it? . . . I've a good memory for names . . . McKenzie, that's it! Adrian's a nice young man,' he added, a shade wistfully.

'Have you any idea where he lives?'

'Two roads up, in Epson Street. I can't say what the

number is, but it's the place with a green front door.'

'It sounds as if he could be my friend . . . Thanks.'

'Glad to be able to help . . . And if you've nothing better to do, come back here and tell me if it really was him.'

Not likely, thought Ansell, as he finished his drink.

Almost all the houses and bungalows in Epson Street were in need of decoration and repair, yet there were so many parked cars, many of them large and less than a year old, that he had considerable difficulty in finding a parking space. He climbed out and locked the doors—as if anyone would consider stealing one of the oldest and most battered cars in sight—and walked along to the house with a green front door. He knocked. The door was opened by Gault, in whose smooth, regularly featured face Ansell saw weakness immediately because he'd always held that a lack of a definite chin denoted a lack of character. 'Is Mr McKenzie in?'

'Are you a split?'

'A what?'

'Wait.' The door was shut.

Split, thought Ansell, was surely slang for a detective; if so, it seemed he might well have found the man he sought.

The door was opened again, this time by McKenzie. 'What d'you bleeding well want?'

'It'll be easier to explain if I come in.'

McKenzie didn't move. After a moment, Ansell stepped inside, easing his way past the large man into the tiny hall. Gault stood in the doorway of the room to the right, his pale blue eyes nervously looking from one to the other of them.

'There's a reward for information about the man who organized the break-in at Highwood Manor,' Ansell said.

'So?'

McKenzie, with that one word, had virtually acknowledged that he understood the reference. Ansell's confidence grew. 'You know what his name is.'

'I don't bloody know nothing.'

'You can identify him because you were the man who helped the other two escape when Poulton had them cornered.'

'He was playing poker when that happened,' said Gault shrilly.

McKenzie shouted: 'Belt up.'

'I was only . . .'

'Just bloody belt up.' McKenzie faced Ansell. 'I weren't near there.'

'I'll give you a thousand pounds if you'll tell me who paid you.'

'No one bloody paid me nothing.'

'In cash.'

'Bugger off.'

'Twelve hundred.'

McKenzie balled his fists again and moved forward.

'No,' shouted Gault. 'You know I can't stand violence.'

Ansell, despite all that had happened, still made the naïve mistake of believing that it was possible to appeal to the other's better nature. 'Maybe you don't know what's happened since Highwood Manor. Three men broke into my house, when my wife and I were asleep. They tied me up and then assaulted her in the most filthy way, even though she's never hurt anyone in the whole of her life; they stripped her and . . . and inserted things into her . . .'

'And she loved every bleeding minute of it and shouted for more.'

Ansell knew an anger so violent that it stripped away all reason and left him with only an elementary desire to smash that vile mouth into silence. He lashed out. The blow never landed. He was hit in the stomach with a violence that doubled him up; a knee slammed into the side of his head to send him sprawling to the floor; and a shoe thudded into his side. Dimly he heard Gault shrilly calling on McKenzie to stop . . .

Nausea tore at his stomach, to add to the other and wildly

growing pains. There was a dark tunnel ahead of him which he longed to enter because it offered oblivion, but perversely it stayed just out of reach . . .

He became aware of hands, soft and soothing, which felt the side of his head; a concerned voice asked him if he was all right and begged him to say that he was. An argument started between the other two about what they were to do with him. Then Gault asked him if he'd come by car and after a while he managed to mumble that he had and the keys were in his pocket. He was dragged to his feet and half supported, half carried out to the Fiesta and painfully eased into the front passenger seat. He didn't lose consciousness, but did lose all sense of time and sequence and he was astonished to find himself in hospital. A nurse undressed him, a doctor examined him, and an X-ray was taken; finally, he was put to bed and given the relief of a sleep-inducing injection.

CHAPTER 23

As he sat on the chair by the side of the end bed in the ward, having listened to Ansell's statement, Brice silently cursed the world for being so brutal, Ansell for being so naïve and, most of all, himself for having originally been so blinded by retributive anger that against orders he had determined to pursue the hit-and-run case.

Ansell broke into his dark thoughts. 'But I really am feeling much better now, thank God!'

'I'm very glad of that.'

'It's getting to be a bit of a habit, isn't it? You coming to see me in hospital.'

'A habit I reckon we need to stop . . . You know, Mr Ansell, whatever you say, we really ought to get in touch with Mrs Ansell.'

'When I'm up and about and then I'll break the news to her myself.'

'I'm sure she'd feel she ought to be here with you.'

'She would, but there's nothing she can do here, is there?'

'But . . .'

'She tried to stop me going to speak to McKenzie. Maybe I don't want to give her the chance of saying, "I told you so".'

A facetious comment, decided Brice, designed to conceal his true thoughts and emotions. And surely those would be bitterness because his attempt to persuade McKenzie to talk had failed and fear for his wife because his actions had made it all too obvious that he had not heeded the savage threats. 'Mr Ansell, I'll leave you in peace very soon, but d'you mind if we just go over something again first? You said you tried to get McKenzie to accept money in return for naming the man who'd given the orders, but he refused, so then you appealed to his better nature. Up to this point, had he threatened you in any way?'

'Not really?'

'But to some extent he had?'

'Well, he did look as if he was going to attack me. Gault shouted at him not to do anything, he couldn't stand violence.'

'McKenzie didn't act more specifically than that?'

'No.'

'You are quite certain of this?'

'Yes. Why d'you keep asking?'

Brice didn't answer directly. 'When he refused your money, you appealed to him on the grounds of humanity, explaining what had happened to your wife?'

'Like the bloody fool I was.'

'Even the biggest fool hopes, Mr Ansell. What happened?'

'I've told you.'

'Please tell me again. It really is very important.'

'He said something utterly vile which made me lose my temper and I tried to attack him.'

'Before he made any obvious and definite move against you?'

'Yes.'

'You can't think of anything he did which led you to believe he was on the point of attacking you?'

'No.'

'After you'd tried to hit him, and failed, he struck you once in the stomach with his fist, once in the head with his knee, and once in the side with his shoe. Did he take his time about doing all that?'

'It was all over in a second. Christ, I didn't know anyone could move so fast!'

Brice sighed. If accused of assault, McKenzie would plead self-defence and although the amount of force he had used had, in the event, proved excessive, on Ansell's evidence it had been employed so quickly that no court would judge he had had time to consider what he was doing. Brice stood. 'That's it, then. Sorry to have bothered you for so long.'

Ansell managed a brief smile, which became a grimace as he altered his position in bed too sharply.

Brice walked down the ward, spoke briefly to the nurse near the door, and then took the lift down to the ground floor. He left through the main entrance and walked round to the carpark, but did not immediately climb into his car; instead he turned, leaned his forearms on the roof, and stared at the Edwardian building whose gaunt lines betrayed its workhouse origins. From the beginning of the case, Ansell had done only what an honest man would do, right up to the point where he had decided to try and bribe McKenzie into naming the man behind the break-ins and even that had been merely a stupid decision, not a dishonest one. Yet he and his wife had suffered appallingly because the police had proved themselves to be incapable of protecting them and from now on, although he might not yet fully have realized the fact, they were under a threat of action even more violent and disgusting than before and the only way they could be certain of escaping this was to uproot themselves and to start a completely new life elsewhere. Why should they be made to suffer? Why should Wright be allowed to escape scot free? Why did the law sometimes protect the criminal rather than the honest man?

Then suddenly it occurred to him that although justice might have been bundled into hiding, there was one way in which she could be dragged back into full view with the blindfold ripped from her eyes. But ironically such success could only be drawn from failure by resorting to illegality . . .

Dora had been married for more years than she cared to remember, but she'd never before seen her husband so obviously uncertain and nervous about how she'd react to a proposal of his. 'I don't understand, Fred. After all, you haven't really told me what it's about.'

'That's because the less you actually know, the better.'

'Then why tell me anything at all?'

'The thing is . . . the thing is, it means going against all the rules; I've never done that before.'

'Why do it now?'

'To correct an injustice.'

'Does that mean you're really saying you've got to do wrong for things to come right?'

He nodded. 'And if I get found out doing it, the shit will close over my head. You'll be badly affected and so, indirectly, will the boys and their families.'

She was silent for a moment, then she said: 'Are you sure that what you want to do is absolutely right?'

'Positive.'

She reached out and gripped his hand and squeezed it. 'That's good enough for me.'

*

Brice saw Drew on the far side of the courtyard at the back of divisional HQ and he called out before hurrying across.

'So where's the fire?' asked Drew.

'I need a word.'

'It sounds important. Have you met a couple of birds who want to share nesting-boxes?'

'You've heard the latest that's happened in the hit-and-run case?'

'You mean that Ansell went along and tried to bribe Scotty to talk? You can't get much stupider than that.'

'He was desperate after what happened to his wife.'

'But to expect Scotty to grass! You might as well expect the old man to smile when the clear-up rates are announced.'

'He wasn't to know it was hopeless.'

'If you ask me, you could fill a book with what he doesn't know about life in the raw.'

'That doesn't make it any less easy for him; makes it worse, really.'

'Ernie, you may know what you're on about, but I'm damned if I do.'

Brice spoke more carefully. 'Earlier on, I had a word with Ansell in hospital. I'd hoped his evidence would prove Scotty had assaulted him, because then we could've put pressure on Scotty to tell us who gave the orders, but he admits he made the first openly aggressive move. And although Scotty used far more force than was justified merely to defend himself, it all happened far too quickly for us to be able to allege he over-reacted deliberately.'

'That leaves him in the clear, then.'

'At the moment, maybe.'

A flurry of wind flicked a strand of hair across Drew's forehead and irritably he brushed it back with his fingers. 'In the clear, period.'

'He's the only lead we have to the top man.'

'Then you're not going to reach him.'

'I reckon we could still do that if . . . Alf, you know what Mrs Ansell went through, don't you?'

'Of course I bloody do.'

'And now she's threatened with worse. Would you move to save her by getting the bastards who were responsible?'

'What sort of a question is that? If I had the chance, I'd personally castrate them.'

'Then you'll help me?'

'Are you tight, or something? Of course I will. I'd be a funny sort of a copper if I wouldn't.'

'It means crossing the line a little.'

Drew's angry, aggressive manner suddenly changed to one of guarded caution. 'Are you suggesting an illegal?'

Brice nodded.

Drew became emphatic once more. 'Forget it.'

'But you've just said . . .'

'Ernie, I'm dead sorry for both of 'em. But that doesn't mean I'm going to be stupid enough to risk sticking my neck on the chopping-block.'

'I need help if my plan's to have a chance.'

'Sorry, but you're on your own.'

'She's been through absolute hell.'

'Maybe, but I'm not risking my career and a spell in prison because of that.'

'Given a bit of luck, it shouldn't ever come to it. We don't have to risk so very much . . .'

'You sound like the woman who had a bastard and tried to excuse herself by saying it was only a very small one . . . No way. And if you've an ounce of brain upstairs, you'll forget the idea. But work out an idea that keeps legal and I'll be with you for twenty-four hours of the day.' He stared challengingly at Brice, then strode off.

Sadly, Brice thought that however unhelpful, Drew's attitude had been the correct one. The moment a policeman moved outside his authority, he ceased to represent the law. And yet what if the law did not allow him to pursue justice . . .?

He walked towards the building, too concerned with his thoughts to note that the wind had risen and the sky was nearly clouded over.

To stand a reasonable chance of succeeding, his plan called for two people to execute it. He'd asked Drew to help, first because Drew had been concerned with the case and knew something of the emotional and physical agonies to which the Ansells had been subjected, secondly because he had always talked belligerently about the need for the rules of evidence to be changed so that fewer guilty men escaped. But as so often proved to be the case, words had come more easily than deeds . . . Brice squared his shoulders. If he couldn't get anyone to help him, then he'd just have to accept the added risk of working on his own.

Half an hour later, having completed some paperwork, he was back in the courtyard and preparing to drive off in one of the CID cars to find a man who was required to make a statement concerning a case in another division, when Higgs hurried up.

Higgs bent down and spoke through the opened window. 'I've been looking for you, Ernie.'

'Yeah? Well I'm in a bit of a rush . . .'

'D'you mind if I get in and have a chat?'

'I suppose not. But keep it short.'

Higgs sat in the front passenger seat. He cleared his throat. 'The thing is, I saw Alf earlier on. He says you've gone round the twist.'

'Like as not, he's right.'

'He says you're stupid enough to be ready to risk everything for people you don't owe anything to.'

Brice said angrily: 'It's time he learned to control his tongue.'

'He didn't say no more than that, no details, but I reckon to know what he was on about. It's the Ansells. There's nothing we can do to get the bastards who assaulted them, is there?'

'Not yet.'

'And after him being beaten up by McKenzie and put in hospital, they must learn he's ignored their threats; so they'll go after him and his wife again. And it won't just be vibrators next time.'

Brice gripped the steering-wheel so hard that his knuckles whitened.

'You've worked out some way of getting at 'em that's not in the rule book, haven't you?'

'You've been thinking too hard. A CID aide's job is to do, not think.'

'Don't try and turn me aside by making a joke of it, Ernie. It's not a joke for you and never has been and nor's it been one for me . . . You wanted Alf to go with you, but he wouldn't touch the idea.'

'He'd good reason to refuse.'

'He refused because he's hard and smart, looks after number one, and only helps someone else if there's no risk to himself.'

'Which adds up to having a whole raft of common sense.'

'That's never the way you think, so don't try to make out it is . . . I'm coming with you.'

'No.'

'Why not?'

'Because although it makes me feel warm inside to have you offer, it makes me cold inside knowing that, if you come, you could be killing your career.'

'You're ready to take that risk.'

'I'm near the end of it anyway.'

'Which gives you a whole lot more to lose. Ernie, you're not the only one with a conscience. And d'you think I haven't thought how I'd feel if it had happened to my mum?'

Brice could no longer refuse him.

CHAPTER 24

Brice braked to a halt outside Highwood Manor. 'You stay here.'

'Why?' demanded Higgs.

'Because it's much better if only one of us goes in.'

'That's all balls! You're still trying to shield me in case something goes wrong.'

'Remember rule number one. Never put your head into a noose unless you have to.'

'Look who's talking!'

'You'll be risking the noose soon enough, so keep clear of it all the time you can.'

Higgs's youthful face, suggesting a greater degree of innocence than had been his even before he joined the force, showed the resentment he felt. But he made no attempt to leave the car.

Brice crossed to the front door and rang the bell. After a brief wait, Jean opened it. He smiled and said: 'D'you remember me—Detective-Constable Brice?'

'Of course I do,' she replied shortly, slightly annoyed that he should have imagined she might not have done.

'Is Mr Poulton back from his holiday yet?'

'No, he isn't.'

'Some people have a good life!' As he spoke, he stepped into the hall, making it seem the natural thing to do so that it did not occur to her that she had not suggested he enter. 'That's a nuisance since I wanted a word with him. Have you any idea when he'll be coming back?'

'No, he's not given me any sort of a date.'

'Then the best thing will be to write to him . . . Last time, you didn't have his address. I imagine he's told you what it is by now?'

'He sent it the other day and told me to forward all his post. D'you know what it cost to do that—over ten quid!'

Brice whistled. 'It comes expensive to be popular . . . Suppose you let me have the address, then, and I'll get in touch with him.'

'It's in the kitchen. Hang on while I go and get it for you.'

As soon as she'd left the hall, Brice went over to the refectory table and took a clean handkerchief from his pocket as he stared down at the several silver ornaments; most were far too large, but there was a water spaniel, no more than two inches high at the shoulder and so finely made that the hairs were distinct, that was not. He picked it up, covered by the handkerchief, and dropped it into his coat pocket. And suddenly it felt as if the coat was being so weighed down to one side, and the pocket was bulging so much, that Jean couldn't fail to notice his theft. For the first time, he fully understood the meaning of the expression, 'crime panic'.

Jean returned to the hall and, showing not the slightest suspicion, handed him a piece of paper. 'Can you read my writing? My son says it's nothing but a scrawl.'

He looked down. 'You tell your son that he's just being cheeky.'

She smiled—for the first time that he could remember. 'I sometimes think he's too cocky for his own good, but with no father alive to keep him down to size, it's difficult.'

He chatted briefly about the young, then said goodbye and left. Once he was seated behind the wheel of the car, he mopped the sweat from his face and neck.

'You look like you've been running a three-minute mile!' said Higgs.

'I feel like I've swallowed a jar of Epsom salts.'

They were fortunate enough to find a parking space at the far end of Epson Street from which there was a good view of McKenzie's house.

'OK?' asked Brice.

Higgs nodded.

Higgs, thought Brice, was beginning to think more closely about the risks he'd soon be running; but his air of determination said that that wasn't deterring his resolution. There was a lot more strength of character in him than a casual acquaintance might suggest. Brice left the car, walked the forty yards to the corner, and turned left. A further two minutes brought him to a row of shops, opposite which was a call-box. He dialled McKenzie's number. He coarsened his voice. 'Is that Scotty?'

'It ain't the bleeding prime minister.'

'Bert says to get along to the hospital right off.'

'Says what?'

'And put your skates on.'

'Who the bleeding hell are you?'

'Tom. Just been along to see him and he's doing his nut on account of the splits.'

'What splits?'

'He says they're giving him a rough time even though he's feeling so crook. Just like those bastards.'

'I don't understand . . .'

'No more do I, but that's what he said to tell you. All right, mate?' Brice replaced the receiver.

He noted the time and then spent a carefully measured ten minutes mooching around the shops—he bought a second-hand paperback Dora would like—even though he was eager to return to Epson Street to find out if his ruse had succeeded; return too soon and McKenzie might see him and that would be that. McKenzie might not be intellectually smart, but few came smarter when it was a question of self-preservation . . .

He returned to the car. 'Well?'

'He drove off about five minutes ago,' said Higgs excitedly.

They walked to McKenzie's house and Brice knocked on the door. Gault opened it. 'Is Scotty in?'

Gault shook his head. 'He's just gone out,' he replied nervously.

'Will he be away long?'

'I can't say. But if you come back . . .'

'No need for that, since we've time to spare. Don't mind us coming in to wait, do you?' Brice stepped inside. Because Gault was essentially weak, he was able to assume a degree of authority that would have been instantly challenged had McKenzie been present.

Gault, obviously uncertain how to act, finally shut the door after Brice and Higgs were in the hall. Brice said: 'Don't mind if we have a sit, do you?' and opened the door of the sitting-room and went in. The television was switched on, showing a video that had been 'paused'. Gault switched off the tape.

'Thirsty weather,' said Brice, as he stood in front of the fireplace.

'It is that,' agreed Higgs.

Gault looked through the window at the street, desperately hoping to see McKenzie, who would know so much better than he how to react to the situation.

'Makes a man real thirsty,' said Brice.

'It does that,' agreed Higgs.

It was not sparkling dialogue, but it had a purpose.

Gault said: 'Would you like something to drink?'

'I wouldn't say no to a jar of lager, that's for sure,' answered Brice.

'And no more would I,' said Higgs.

Gault left the room.

Brice went over to the mantelpiece and put on it the silver water spaniel, next to a framed picture of a country cottage made from different coloured sands. He was seated in one of the armchairs when Gault returned with a tray on which were two tankards and a whisky glass. He offered the tray to them in turn.

Brice raised his glass, then put it down. 'Just before we

relax and get social, maybe it'd be best if we sort something out. We came for a chat with Scotty—nothing serious. But while you were out of the room, getting the drinks, I saw something interesting on the mantelpiece, there. Isn't that right?' he asked Higgs.

'Dead right,' replied Higgs.

'You know what I mean, don't you?'

'No.' In his apprehension, Gault slopped some of the whisky out of the glass and it ran down his hand towards the sleeve of his shirt; hurriedly, he brought a handkerchief from his pocket and mopped it up.

'Kept it, I suppose, instead of melting it down, because it's a lovely piece of work. That does you credit, artistically speaking, but not from the point of view of common sense.' Brice shook his head as if he couldn't understand how anyone could willingly have taken such a risk.

'What are you on about?' demanded Gault shrilly, becoming frantic because he could not identify the danger that was so clearly threatening him.

'The silver dog over there, of course. Why, have you something else around you wouldn't want us to see?'

Gault stared across at the mantelpiece. 'There's no dog . . .' he began, then stopped abruptly. He stood, crossed over, picked up the dog. 'This isn't ours.'

'That's true enough.'

'But it's the first time I've ever seen it.'

'So are you suggesting it walked here of its own accord?'

'I swear I've never clapped eyes on it before.'

'No more have I, but I know exactly where it came from.' He half turned. 'Would you reckon to know as well?'

'I would,' answered Higgs.

'It's the silver dog Mr Poulton had nicked the night Scotty and his two mates broke into Highwood Manor.'

'They never took anything,' Gault shouted.

'But you're agreeing that they were there?'

'I didn't mean it like that,' he said frantically. 'Scotty was with me all night.'

'Are you now saying you were there with them?'

'You've got me all confused.'

'Because you can't remember the lies you were supposed to tell? . . . Mr Poulton gave us a full description of the silver dog. Looking at it now, I'd say there's no doubt.'

'Not even a shadow of a doubt,' agreed Higgs faithfully.

'So you're knowingly in possession of stolen property.'

'You've got to believe . . .' began Gault.

Brice said: 'It's funny how the law still sees the theft of property as real serious, when it doesn't seem to worry much about so many other things. You can mug an old woman and hope for a suspended sentence, but break into a house and nick something and you're taken to the cleaners. Someone once told me it's on account of history that people are valued less than things in law. Could be. History's got its funny side . . . Bad luck for you that it has, of course. Even receiving this stolen dog will make any judge see red.'

'You can't prove anything . . .'

'When Mr Poulton testifies that that's his dog and we testify that we found it on your mantelpiece, and your dabs are discovered on it, everything's proved. Of course, you may be lucky enough to come up before a soft judge and escape with just a trio and then, with good behaviour and so on, that means you could be back outside within a year. But it'll be a long, long year. You know what it'll be like for you, don't you? Hundreds of men starved of sex and you turn up, to start 'em all panting. They'll be like a pack of dogs after a bitch on heat. Desperate for a cuddle. And the unlucky ones will end up frustrated and like as not will blame you and try to take their frustrations out on you. I always remember what happened a couple of years back at Blackhurst Jail. A young, handsome bloke—as a matter of interest, he looked very much like you—was sent down and when he arrived at the nick there was a real scramble among the lads; one of 'em, who got left out, was a nasty piece of work from up north who was in for manslaughter and he got close to this bloke and used a knife he'd made in the workshops so fast that before the screws could pull him off, he'd made the poor devil look like minced beef. Took a team of surgeons to save him and from all accounts he's never seen cause to thank 'em because his face got it worst and instead of looking like Adonis, he ended up like Quasimodo . . . Frankly, you strike me as someone who can't take violence so I'm thinking things could become real nasty for you . . .'

'No!' shouted Gault. He looked as if about to cry.

'They're worse than animals. And it shouldn't happen to anyone, least of all to a peaceful, artistic kind of a bloke like you. But there's nothing we can do. Unless . . .'

'Unless what?'

'Well, unless you cooperate with us so as we could rightly forget we'd ever seen the silver dog here.'

Despite his mental panic, Gault finally realized that he was being blackmailed to give evidence. He longed to find the courage to resist, but his mind was too filled with the horror of the savagery that Brice had just painted. 'What d'you want?' he demanded hoarsely.

'The name of the man who gave the orders for the break-in at Highwood Manor.'

'But I don't know it.'

'That's bad luck, isn't it. Bad luck for you.'

'I swear that all Scotty's ever mentioned is someone called Wright . . .'

'He'll do. So now write out a statement which you can sign.' Brice brought his notebook out of his pocket.

'I can't. I won't.'

'What a pity! You really would rather be sliced up by a homemade knife?

'You bastards!' Gault shrieked, now almost as terrified by their demands as by their threats.

'Sometimes it takes a bastard to catch a bastard . . . Write: "I have heard Scotty McKenzie say that Samuel Wright was the man who paid him and his two companions to break into Highwood Manor." And don't forget to put the date as well as to sign it.'

Gault hesitated, then, with a small cry of despair, took the notebook and pencil and wrote.

Brice pocketed the notebook. He went over to the mantelpiece, took a handkerchief from his pocket, picked up the silver dog. 'I'll see this is returned to its owner. And if ever you feel like denying your statement, remember that your dabs will be on it.' He pocketed the dog, then led the way over to the doorway. He turned. 'One last word. You'll know better than me what kind of a temper Scotty's got. So if I were you, I wouldn't let him know that you've shopped him. Best to say nothing about our little visit. That way, you won't have to leave here in an ambulance.'

CHAPTER 25

Mumford, having read Gault's signed statement, looked up. 'How did you get hold of this?'

'He was eager to see justice done,' replied Brice.

'In a pig's eye!'

'Then does it matter? All that's important is that it finally gives us the clout to ask for a search warrant to Wright's house.'

Mumford spoke slowly. 'When I was doing my basic training, there was an inspector who used to lecture us on the ethos and morals of police work. Boring as hell, but I always remember one thing he said. Become personally involved in a case and you're in trouble because you can no longer see where your duty lies.'

'I'd put things the other way round.'

'You would, you bloody fool!' Mumford snapped. But there was a measure of reluctant admiration in his voice.

The four detectives left the car and walked across to the front door of Wright's house. Drew rang the bell; there was no response.

'See if the gardener's around at the back,' ordered Detective-Inspector Redstart-Havers.

Drew checked the back garden, then returned to report that there was no sign of anyone.

'All right. Open up.'

Mumford produced a bunch of skeleton keys and in turn tried them in the lock. The fifth one turned the tumblers, but the door still refused to open, showing it was bolted. They walked round the house. There were two back doors and the second one was not bolted. Once inside, they went through to the kitchen and from there into the large, two-storeyed hall. 'Two of you upstairs,' ordered the DI.

Drew and Brice climbed the wide staircase, at the head of which was a landing with a passage leading off on either side. Drew sniffed. 'God, what a stink!'

They found the bodies of a man and woman in the main bedroom; each had been gagged, bound, and shot.

The pathologist, a short, stubby man with a round, full face and thick, curling lips, came out of the bedroom, followed by his secretary. He walked along to the landing where the detective-superintendent from county HQ was talking to Redstart-Havers. Ignoring the dictates of good manners, he brusquely interrupted their conversation. 'I've finished, so the bodies can be moved to the morgue.' He brought out a small tortoiseshell box from his coat pocket, opened the lid, and helped himself to a generous pinch of snuff; popular belief had it that it was his addiction to snuff which rendered him immune to smells that sickened others. 'They were both killed by the muzzle of a gun, pointing upwards, being held against the small of the neck. I will conduct the post-mortems as soon as possible, so please don't keep bothering me for the results.' He nodded a goodbye and went past them and down the stairs, his secretary, a much shorter-legged man, having to move quickly in order to keep up with him.

Ten minutes after the bodies, wrapped in body-bags, had been carried out of the house, Redstart-Havers showed an empty, scrumpled-up cigarette pack to the detective-superintendent. 'This has just been found in a rubbish-bin in the kitchen. From the address of the company, it comes from Beirut; the writing's in French and also in what could be Arabic.'

The detective-superintendent looked down at the pack. 'Do we know if either Wright or his wife were smokers?'

'No, sir.'

'Check with the gardener when you've found him. And also ask him whether he knows if either of them had recently been abroad to that part of the world.'

For no readily discernible reason, although the bullet which had killed Wright had fragmented beyond the possibility of reconstruction, that which killed his wife had not. Photographs and measurements were taken of the number and width of grooves impressed on the bullet and the direction and degree of twist of the spiral, with special reference to the minute and unique identifying marks; comparisons were made with records of bullets from past crimes and details were sent to Interpol.

Interpol reported that the bullet had been fired from the same gun, a P.38 Walther, as had killed Ms'aruf, the then Saudi Arabian oil minister, two and a half years previously. Contemporary reports, never substantiated, had named a terrorist who worked under the *nom de guerre* of Guernica. Over the years, no less than six known terrorists had been identified as Guernica; it was believed that this was because of a sustained and clever disinformation campaign. Guernica was a man of extreme left-wing political views who had on one certain occasion had connections with Al Est. That group had, for years, been working for the overthrow of the Saudi Arabian ruling family.

Guernica's known victims numbered eight, five of whom had been Middle Eastern politicians of moderate persuasions whose deaths had caused turmoil in politically sensitive areas. Photographs, of regrettably poor quality, of four of the six terrorists named as Guernica were forwarded; there were neither photographs nor worthwhile descriptions of the remaining two men.

Brice parked his car outside No. 7, walked up the path to the front door, and rang the bell. Ansell opened the door. 'More questions?' he asked wearily.

'You'll be glad to hear, not this time. It's good to see you back home. How are you feeling?'

'Slightly more human than the last time you saw me.'

'And is Mrs Ansell all right?'

'Yes, but she's becoming very impatient because she wants to return.'

'She can, as soon as she likes.'

'How's that? . . . How can it be safe?'

'Largely, Mr Ansell, because you had the courage to go on and on and eventually tried to bribe McKenzie. You see, what happened when you did that gave us the chance we needed . . . But maybe I could explain things from the beginning?'

Ansell asked him in, apologizing for not already having done so. They went through to the sitting-room where the fire was lit but the lights were not yet switched on, so that the room was filled with leaping shadows.

'As you know,' said Brice, 'for some time we'd been reasonably certain a man called Wright had been driving the hit-and-run car, but we'd been unable to find the proof of this. Now, when a criminal goes to unusual and potentially dangerous lengths to avoid being questioned by the police, it's a safe bet that either he has just been, or is about to be, engaged in a major crime. Wright tried to persuade you and Mr Poulton not to give us any evidence concerning the accident, or not to stand by that which you'd already given, because he believed you could provide us with sufficient evidence to ensure that we'd be entitled to investigate him in depth—you have to remember that a criminal is always under the disadvantage of not being certain how much the police know and this almost invariably leads him to overrate their knowledge. Now, we can see that in order to hide his part in the hit-and-run, his best bet would have been to do absolutely nothing and meet any police inquiries with a flat denial; but he assumed that you could provide far more conclusive evidence than you could and must therefore be silenced. First, he tried bribery, then threats, then violence. Each time he failed to stop you, his actions obviously had to become more extreme if they were to stand any chance of succeeding. And it was because of this that he and his wife were murdered.'

Ansell gasped.

'To understand why, I need to go back in time. On the day of the hit-and-run, the coastguards became interested in a motor-cruiser. The day was misty and visibility was poor, so the boat could only be followed on radar. Ten miles out to sea, it was observed to approach another craft. I'm sure I don't need to tell you that there's still a lot of smuggling goes on and that when a couple of craft meet in mid-Channel, it's quite possible they're engaged in some form of smuggling. In this particular case, though, the two craft passed each other at slow speed and so it was assumed that their close encounter was fortuitous. In fact, a man had been transferred from one to the other on an inflatable— which was too small to show up on the radar—while they kept moving to disarm any suspicion.

'Wright, with the man he'd picked up, docked and began the drive to his home, but on the way there was an accident. He didn't dare stop because the man was a noted terrorist.

'During his stay at Wright's home, the terrorist was clearly able to judge how seriously Wright was over-reacting to the police inquiries and how his actions were likely to provoke the one thing he was trying to avoid: a really thorough investigation which would expose the terrorist's presence. So he decided that for his own safety he must murder Wright and his wife.'

'Then I . . . In a kind of a way, I'm responsible for their murders?'

'In no way. There can be no doubt that the decision was merely put forward in time. Had Wright been a degree smarter and less dazzled by the large amount of money he'd been offered, he'd have realized at the beginning that since he and his wife must learn so much about the terrorist, their deaths must be projected if the terrorist's anonymity was to be maintained . . . Which brings me back to where I started and to repeat that it's now perfectly safe for Mrs Ansell to return home. With Wright dead, there'll be no more attempts to frighten you into silence.'

Ansell checked that the two outside doors were bolted, chained, and locked, and all window catches secured; it was a routine that would be with him for the rest of his life.

Upstairs, Brenda was unpacking her suitcase and as he entered the bedroom, she looked up. 'It's wonderful to be back!' She smiled, then carried a couple of blouses over to the drawers in her cupboard. 'Mike . . .'

'Yes?'

'You really are glad to have me back, aren't you?'

'Do you have to ask?'

'Then what's the matter? You're surely not still blaming yourself for everything?'

'I . . . I suppose I am,' he answered reluctantly. 'I can't

stop thinking that nothing would have happened to you if I'd not insisted on sticking by all my ridiculous principles.'

'They weren't, and aren't, ridiculous.'

'Aren't they? I saw myself as too honourable to accept a bribe.'

'Do you think I'd love you half as much as I do if you weren't?'

'But if I'd accepted it, you wouldn't have suffered.'

'One can't always prevent suffering. If you'd kept the thousand pounds, I'd have been all right, but the police wouldn't have learned that the terrorist was in the country, probably planning a political murder, and they wouldn't have taken all the precautions that they're going to now and so maybe lots of innocent people would have suffered.'

'I don't care about anyone else, only you.'

'What happened to me was unpleasant but of no lasting account; it was nothing compared to the suffering of people hideously injured by a bomb.'

He wondered at the depths of her love. He went over, kissed her, and tried to put into words his feelings for her. And later, there was no need for him to apologize.

The inspector, who was in plain clothes, followed the comisario out on to the hotel patio. Newly out from a cold and wet London, he stared at the sun-drenched gardens filled with the colours of roses, hibiscus, plumbago, lantana, chrysanthemums and bougainvillaea; at the orange trees with fruit that was just beginning to change colour; and at the bay whose waters were a blue that in England was seen only on travel posters. A waiter carrying a tray of empty glasses began to pass them, then came to an abrupt halt as the comisario spoke. He pointed with his free hand at one of the wrought-iron tables with overhead sun umbrellas that were set to the right of the stone steps which led down to the beach.

When they reached the table, the inspector said: 'Mr

Poulton? My companion is Comisario Lluerca of the Spanish police and my name is Inspector Morrit.'

'It sounds as if you're a long way from home, so sit down and have a drink.' Poulton signalled to a waiter who hurried over and took the orders. He turned to the woman who was with him. 'Tell you what, Sandra, you go and change so that you're ready to head for town.'

She pouted, annoyed at being sent away, but did not argue. As she walked across the patio, she was watched by almost every man in sight.

Poulton settled back in the chair and his hard, handsome face was outside the shade of the umbrella and the sun glinted on his dark glasses. 'So what can I do for you?'

'You were an eye-witness to a hit-and-run near Ingleton towards the end of September, weren't you?' answered Morrit.

'In general terms, yes; in specific ones, no; it had all happened before I reached the actual scene.'

'But the car had passed you earlier on and you saw the passenger in it. What I'd like to do is to show you some photos and for you to say whether you can identify any one of them as that passenger.'

The waiter brought the drinks and set the glasses on the table. Poulton waited until he'd left, then said: 'Have you come over from England just to ask me to do that?'

'Yes.'

'Then it obviously has to be important.'

'We've reason to believe that the passenger was a terrorist who had just been smuggled into the country.'

Poulton silently whistled. Then he said thoughtfully: 'Hence the bribe . . . The one the other man was offered . . . and the break-in at my place. Is this terrorist still in England?'

'Probably.'

'Do you know what his target is?'

'We can only speculate at the moment.'

'What's his nationality?'

'All we can say is, probably Middle Eastern.'

'You don't seem to know much for certain.'

'Frankly, we don't.'

Poulton drank, replaced his glass on the table. 'Let's have a look at the photos, then.' He was handed four and he looked through them. 'They could be a lot clearer!'

'The subjects would have been rather shy of having their photos taken,' replied the inspector drily.

'Let's get one thing straight. I'd no reason to take particular note of the passenger and in any case he was only in sight for a second.'

'That's understood.'

'But I'm good on faces and I'm reasonably certain it was this one.' He indicated what was now the top photograph of the four.

Twenty minutes and a round of drinks later, the three men left the patio and went into the hotel. Poulton said goodbye to the policemen, then took the lift up to his suite on the third floor.

Sandra, wearing only a pair of bikini pants, was standing in front of one of the cupboards in the bedroom. 'I don't know what to wear,' she said in an aggrieved tone. 'I put the new skirt on, but I don't feel pink today. And you don't like me in trousers.'

'Then go as you are.' He went over to the bed and sat on it, picked up the telephone receiver and asked the hotel switchboard operator for a London number.

'Who are you ringing?' she asked, as she brought out a patterned frock from the cupboard and stared at it.

'Father Christmas.'

'Then you can tell him I want—'

'Keep the list short; he's only one sleigh.' He waited impatiently for the connection to be made. Only that morning he had read in *The Times* that the Saudi Arabian oil minister was visiting Britain in two days' time to discuss the possibility of making fresh attempts to stabilize the price of oil in the long term. The aim of most terrorists was to create the maximum amount of turmoil and the assassination of another Saudi Arabian oil minister would cause that (as would even the news that this had been projected); such turmoil would almost certainly be reflected in the price of crude oil. So oil futures bought now could show a dramatic profit . . . He smiled sardonically. Wouldn't the mugs of the world choke if they ever learned that it was his original acceptance of a thousand-pound bribe which was to lead to his making a fortune . . .